"Come on, Kel! You can do it!" Kenan shouted down the stairwell.

Kel, dressed in full mountain-climbing gear, finally turned the corner up to the seventy-third floor. He struggled with his enormous backpack. "Are we almost there? This is getting heavy," Kel complained.

"You shouldn't have brought so much stuff. What do you have in there?"

"Let's see," Kel began, as he rummaged through his backpack. "Weights . . ."

Kenan had difficulty understanding why Kel needed to bring weights up to the top of the Sears Tower with him.

"Hey, maybe that's what's makin' your backpack so heavy. You think?" Kenan asked sarcastically. "Did you bring any food?"

Kel pulled out a huge glass bowl of fruit. "I got fruit," he offered.

"Did you have to bring the big ol' heavy bowl?" asked Kenan.

"I don't want my backpack full o' loose fruits!" exclaimed Kel, thinking this was perfectly reasonable thinking. He then reached into his backpack and pulled out a juicer. "Oh, I also brought a juicing machine to juice my fruits."

"Look, Kel, isn't that *my parents'* juicer?"

"My parents wouldn't let me bring theirs," replied Kel.

Look for these Nickelodeon® books:

Good Burger™
Good Burger™ 2 Go
Kenan & Kel™: Aw, Here It Goes!
All That™: Fresh Out the Box

Available from MINSTREL Books

NICKELODEON®

KENAN & KEL™

AW, HERE IT GOES!

Steve Freeman

Based on the teleplays "Doing Things the Heming Way" and "Dial 'O' for 'Oops'" by Kevin Kopelow & Heath Seifert and "Foul Bull" by Steve Freeman

A MINSTREL® BOOK

Published by POCKET BOOKS
New York   London   Toronto   Sydney   Tokyo   Singapore

This book is a work of fiction. Names, characters, places and incidents are products of the author's imagination or are used fictitiously. Any resemblance to actual events or locales or persons, living or dead, is entirely coincidental.

A MINSTREL PAPERBACK *Original*

A Minstrel Book published by
POCKET BOOKS, a division of Simon & Schuster Inc.
1230 Avenue of the Americas, New York, NY 10020

Copyright © 1998 by Viacom International Inc. All rights reserved.
Based on the Nickelodeon series entitled "Kenan & Kel."

ISBN: 0-671-02428-0

First Minstrel Books printing October 1998

10 9 8 7 6 5 4 3 2

NICKELODEON, Kenan & Kel, and all related titles,
logos and characters are trademarks of Viacom International Inc.

A MINSTREL BOOK and colophon are registered
trademarks of Simon & Schuster Inc.

Cover photography by Tom Hurst

Printed in the U.S.A.

Many thanks to Kevin Kopelow, Heath Seifert,
Brian Robbins, Dan Schneider, and Sal Maniaci.

THE REALLY SERIOUS ADVENTURES OF KENAN AND KEL

Kenan and Kel walk out in front of the red curtain on the *Kenan and Kel* stage.

"Hey, everybody! I'm Kel," says Kel to a studio full of empty seats.

"And I'm Kenan," says Kenan to no one in particular. Kel looks out at all the empty seats. "Hey, Kenan. Where is everyone?"

"Don't worry about that," replies Kenan.

"But, Kenan," Kel continues, "how are we gonna do our television show with no one in the audience?"

"This is not our television show, Kel!"

"Then what are we doin' out here on stage if it's not time for our television program?" says Kel with a look of utter confusion. This look, Kenan thinks to himself, is not an unfamiliar one for Kel. Kel is confused more than anyone Kenan has ever known. Sometimes he's confused and he doesn't even know it. In fact, Kel is confused so often, Kenan actually considers renaming him the Master of Confusion. He decides to do this now.

"Kel," Kenan announces, "I am officially renaming you the Master of Confusion."

"Far out." Kel beams with delight. "I've always wanted to be a master of something. My momma will be so proud!" He begins to shout and jump up and down. "I made it, momma! I'm somebody!"

"Congratulations," says Kenan.

"You're welcome!" Kel yelps with glee. "But that still doesn't explain how come we're here on the *Kenan and Kel* stage with nobody in the audience, and it's Saturday night."

"We don't always have to be on TV every time we tell stories, do we?" asks Kenan impatiently.

Kel considers this for a moment. "Well, I guess not," he replies.

"Okay. Now let's get started. The people are waiting."

"What people?" Kel again looks out toward the empty seats.

"Use your imagination, Kel."

"Hey, what's all this 'Kel' stuff? I thought I was the Master of . . . of . . ." Kel is confused again.

". . . Confusion."

"Yeah, that's it." Kel is relieved to remember the rest of the cool name Kenan has just given him. "But, I've been thinking . . . do you think I can be the *President* of Confusion? I like that better."

"Man, you can be the President of Confusion, the King of Confusion, or the Executive Producer of Confusion, for all I care!" Kenan offers.

"Good," says Kel. "Then I'll be the *Princess* of Confusion. Let's start the show."

"Now, wait a minute, Princess," Kenan cautions. "This isn't our TV show. It's a *book.*"

"A book?" Kel is surprised. "You mean like *The Pretty Little Pony* or *Andy the Anteater Goes to Jail?*"

"Yeah, sort of," answers Kenan. "And the audience are all the people who are reading what you and me are tellin' 'em in the book. Get it?"

"Not at all," Kel says cheerfully.

"Well, you'll get it as we go along." Kenan feels kind of worn out and takes a deep breath. He usually feels this way after a conversation with Kel, and since Kenan and Kel spend a lot of time together, Kenan feels worn out quite often.

"What are we gonna tell the people in our book, Kenan?" Kel asks.

"Well," begins Kenan, "some people must be curious about what it's like to *be* Kenan and Kel."

"I'm not," says Kel.

"Of course, *you're* not, bran muffin!" exclaims Kenan. "'Cuz you're Kel. You already know all about what it's like to be you. The people who *aren't* you are the ones who are curious."

"Are there a lot of people who aren't me?" Kel asks earnestly.

"Quite a few," replies Kenan. "And it would be refreshing to start hangin' out with *them.*"

"I don't understand, Kenan. What are the people curious about?"

"You know," replies Kenan, "personal stuff like our hobbies and our feelings and things like that."

"Oh, *feelings.*" Kel suddenly has a rare expression of understanding on his face. "I've got an all-time *fa*-vo-rite feeling. Ya know that feeling when ya drink orange soda so fast, it feels like it's about to come out your nose?"

"Maybe we should get away from feelings and concentrate on something else," Kenan decides. "I have an idea."

"Oh no!" says Kel, suddenly frightened and concerned.

"Look," Kenan says, in a calming voice so that Kel won't be so scared. "Since we're right here on the *Kenan and Kel* stage, and since this stage is our favorite place for telling about our escapades—"

"'Escapades'?" Kel interrupts. "Kenan, we can't even skate."

"'*Escapades,*' not '*Ice* Capades.'" Kenan is becoming more frustrated than he ever thought possible. "It means 'adventures.' You and me have had some really serious adventures, and we're gonna tell the people about some of them."

"Ooh!" shouts Kel. "Like the time you fell—?"

"No!" Kenan quickly interrupts. "Not that adventure. We'll tell the people about other adventures."

"Okay," Kel agrees, much to Kenan's relief. "The only problem is, every time we've ever had an adventure, we've gotten into trouble."

"That's okay," Kenan reassures Kel. "People like to hear about other people's trouble."

"That's true," Kel agrees. "And trouble is something you and me suuuuurre are good at causin'."

"Yep. Why, I guess you can say we've turned gettin' into trouble into an art form. And the beauty of it is, it's art that we never mean to create."

"Yeah," says Kel as if he's just made a great discovery. "It always seems to happen 'accidentally.' I wonder if dudes like Michelangelo, Picasso, Coolio, and all those other artists who end with 'o' create their art 'accidentally.'"

"I don't know," says Kenan. "But I think there's something else that's interesting about all the trouble we get into."

"What's that, Kenan?"

"Well," says Kenan thoughtfully. "Maybe the way it works is, *sometimes* the more trouble you get into, the better the adventures you're having."

"So we must have some really fine adventures."

"Yeah, we're the Earls of Adventure!" exclaims Kenan. They both laugh and slap each other a high five.

"But, wait a minute," says Kel. "If I'm an Earl of Adventure, can I still be the Princess of Confusion?"

"I think so," responds Kenan, a little confused himself.

"Great. This has been a really good day for me," Kel says, smiling ear-to-ear.

"But . . ." begins Kenan, who now seems bothered by something.

"But what?"

"But . . . is having adventures and getting into trouble all there is to life?" says Kenan, suddenly philosophical. This disturbs Kel a great deal.

"Why are you suddenly philosophical, Kenan? I just hate it when you get suddenly philosophical."

"Listen, Kel. We're getting older," Kenan says. "Maybe we need to start setting some more serious goals."

"Scoring goals?" says Kel, in an annoyed tone. "Kenan, I told you I don't ice skate, so that can only mean I don't play hockey either."

"Not *scoring* goals, Stanley Cup head!" Kenan yells. *"Setting* goals. And that's what our first story is gonna be about—setting goals and going after them."

"Kenan, I know what your problem is." Kel puts his arm around his obviously misguided pal. "You read too many books with big words. You really oughta' pick up *The Pretty Little Pony*. It's good light reading and it doesn't leave you thinking so much. Too much thinkin' can be hard on your brain."

"Books," says Kenan. "That gives me an idea."

"But, Kenan," pleads Kel. "People shouldn't be getting ideas from books!"

"I'll see ya after the story." With that, Kenan walks off the stage.

"Kenan? What about our adventure?" screams Kel. "What's gonna happen to us? Kenan?" Realizing Kenan has already walked away, Kel shakes his head in frustration. "Aw, here it goes!" shouts Kel, and he runs off after Kenan.

"DOING THINGS THE HEMING WAY"

Rigby's Grocery Store will never be a supermarket. It's just a small neighborhood grocery store. Small enough, in fact, that Kenan Rockmore spent his working hours reading a book when there were no customers for him to help.

It was a normal day like any other day at Rigby's. Kenan sat behind the counter in his blue Rigby's apron reading a book. Kel Kimble was there too, making a nuisance out of himself. There are some things one could always be sure of finding at Rigby's, things like produce, dairy products, cereal, and Kel.

"Hey, Kenan? You mind if I make a sandwich for lunch?" Kel asked as he walked over to the bread section.

"Uh, it's about five-thirty," Kenan responded without looking up from his book.

At that moment Chris Potter, the store manager, walked in, wearing his gray manager's apron and holding a freshly hand-painted sign. The sign was supposed to say "Three Bananas For A Dollar." However, instead of writing the word, "bananas," Chris painted a picture of what was supposed to be a bunch of bananas.

"Hey, guys. Look at the sign I painted! I call it 'Three Bananas For A Dollar.' I'm quite the artiste if I do say so myself," Chris proudly proclaimed.

Kenan, however, could not be bothered. He was completely absorbed in his book.

"Kenan? Hello? What do you think of my painting?" Chris demanded. Finally, Kenan looked up from his reading and squinted at Chris's masterpiece.

"Three baseball mitts for a dollar?" he asked.

"No! Three *bananas* for a dollar," Chris said.

"Looks like a baseball mitt to me," said Kenan. He resumed reading his book.

"Well," said Chris, his feelings somewhat hurt, "obviously you know nothing about fruit art." Chris was a sensitive, sometimes cranky, store manager. He was dedicated to his store and took pride in his displays, no matter how bad they were.

"Yeah," Kenan replied, "at school I'm always skippin' my fruit-art class."

"What are you reading there?" Chris asked.

"I'm reading about Ernest Hemingway, the great American author," replied Kenan grandly.

"Oh, Ernest Hemingway. I've read all of his books," Chris bragged. *For Whom the Bell Tolls, The Old Man and the Sea.* They're all classics."

"And I've seen all his movies," Kel chimed in. *"Ernest Goes to Camp, Ernest Saves Christmas, Ernest—"*

"Kel," began Chris, somewhat amazed at Kel's ignorance, "I think that may be a different Ernest."

Kel simply stared at Chris's sign. "Three octopuses for a dollar?" he asked.

"No!" replied Chris, extremely frustrated. "Three *bananas* for a dollar!"

"But it looks like an octopus," Kel insisted.

"It does not! It's a bunch of bananas!" Chris was now very insulted. "I'm going outside to hang my sign!" With that, he stormed out of the store.

Kel, in the meantime, ripped open a package of lunch meat (which he never paid for. Kel never pays for anything at Rigby's) and began making a sandwich.

"Check this out, Kel," said Kenan, his eyes still riveted to his book. "Ernest Hemingway said that for him to be a complete person, he had to do three things: 'plant a tree, bear a son, and fight a bull.'"

"Well, then Ernest Hemingway's an idiot," replied Kel as he walked over to the produce section.

Kenan looked up from his book and followed Kel, determined to give him an appreciation for something besides lunch meat and orange soda. Well, as far as orange soda was concerned, for Kel, it was far more than an appreciation. It was a deep love. It was an obsession. An addiction. Kenan was convinced that Kel must have drunk orange soda instead of milk when he was a baby, and he was certain that if Kel had his way, there would be no water—only orange soda. *He'd swim in it, shower with it, even brush his teeth with it,* Kenan thought. But it would be Kel's sandwich Kenan would have to compete with now.

"No! Don't you see?" Kenan was suddenly excited. "Hemingway is saying that we need to set our own goals and go for 'em! It's a positive thing."

Kel was only interested in his sandwich as he began adding lettuce. "Aww, how could you get something so positive from a schoolbook?"

Kenan, now very irritated, grabbed Kel's sandwich from him. "How did you get something so free from my store?" Kenan demanded, waving the sandwich in Kel's face. "Kel, isn't there something that you always wanted to achieve in life?"

"Right now, my stomach would like to achieve that sandwich," he replied with hunger in his eyes.

"Isn't there something *more* important you want?" Kenan asked.

Kel took a moment and thought real hard. "I always wanted to meet an Eskimo," he answered truthfully.

Kenan felt this was a weird thing to want, but he wasn't about to argue with Kel. "Okaay," said Kenan with a tone of reluctant acceptance. "Well, I'm going to set goals for myself so I can be a complete person like Ernest Hemingway."

"Hey, Kenan. Whatever happened to Ernest Hemingway?"

"Oh, he's dead," Kenan replied casually before taking a big bite out of Kel's sandwich.

"I don't wanna be *that* complete," said Kel.

Roger Rockmore was a big, tall, hard-working, bald man. An air-traffic controller at the airport, Roger had a high-pressure job telling people when and where to fly. He looked forward to the peace and quiet of his home after a hard day's work. Sheryl Rockmore, a loving and dedicated wife and mother, cuddled with Roger on the couch in front of the TV. They had rented a movie, and were happily eating a bowl of popcorn, when Kenan and Kel walked in.

"Listen, Kel," Kenan continued their conversation, "Hemingway was sayin' you need to accomplish your goals before you get all old, boring, and bald-headed."

"Kenan!" Sheryl Rockmore said. "Don't talk about your father like that!"

Roger was frustrated. Not so much due to the accidental insult, but more because Kel was in his home again. It wasn't that Roger didn't like his son's friend. It's just that Kel always managed to get on Roger's nerves. Well, okay. Roger didn't particularly like Kel.

"Popcorn!" shouted Kel, noticing the bowl of popcorn on the coffee table. He jumped onto the sofa right between Roger and Sheryl.

"Help yourself," said Roger, sarcastically.

"Whatcha watchin'?" asked Kel, with an ear-to-ear smile and a mouth full of the Rockmores' popcorn.

"Hopefully," Roger replied, "we're gonna be watchin' *you going home.*"

"We're watching a classic old movie called *Casablanca*," said Sheryl, ignoring her husband's frustration. "This is the first movie Kenan's father and I ever saw together."

"Ooh, then this movie must be ancient!" exclaimed Kel. "Cavemen probably watched this movie."

"Don't you kids have anything to do?" Roger asked.

Kenan wasted no time telling his parents about their grand plan. "Me and Kel are setting life goals for ourselves," he announced proudly.

"That's what Ernest Hemingway did," Kel chimed in.

Sheryl was impressed.

"You're looking at the new Kenan!" proclaimed her son. "The thrill-seekin', risk-takin', globe-trottin' Kenan!"

"If only you could be the homework-doin', bed-makin', room-cleanin' Kenan," replied Sheryl.

Ignoring his mother, Kenan continued with his grand declarations. "I have chosen my goals," Kenan began. "I will do three things: I will save somebody's life! I will declare my love to a girl! And I will climb something real adventurous like . . . Mount Everest!"

"I want to meet an Eskimo," added Kel.

"Well, Kenan," said Sheryl supportively, "whatever you want to do, your father and I are behind you one hundred percent."

"And, Kel," Roger added, "we're behind *you* fifty percent."

Kel was grateful. No one had ever been behind him fifty percent before. "Thanks. Well, I was goin' home, but I think I'll stay here and watch the movie with your daddy," he announced.

Roger was not pleased about this decision. "Aw, you don't wanna do that," he said.

"Sure I do!" Kel insisted. "I wanna start doing things I've never done before, and I've never seen this old movie."

Roger pretended to yawn. "Well, uh . . . it's just that we're going to bed pretty soon and . . ."

"Well, if you're going to sleep," said Kel, walking over to the VCR and popping the tape out, "then you won't mind if I watch this movie at my house."

"But . . . but . . ." Roger was at a loss for words. He pointed helplessly at the VCR.

"Oh yeah, thanks," said Kel, gratefully. "I don't have a VCR." With that, Kel grabbed the VCR and left the Rockmore home.

"He took our videotape, and our VCR. It all happened so fast." Roger was in a daze, as his wife comforted him.

"Do you want me to call him back?" Kenan offered.

"No!" shouted Roger and Sheryl, both frightened by the idea of Kel coming back.

"Chrrrriiisss!!" Kenan screamed as he saw the Rigby's manager climb on a stepladder to place items on a high shelf. "Your shoe's untied!"

"Huh?" said Chris as he looked down at his shoe, noticing it was, in fact, untied. "Oh, thanks." He bent down to tie his shoe.

"Hey! I guess I just saved your life," declared Kenan.

"Uhm no you didn't," argued Chris.

"Come on! You could've tripped over your shoelace and busted your head wide open. Admit it! I just saved your life!" Kenan shouted as if he were trying to convince not only Chris, but himself.

"Have you been adding sugar to your Sugar Frosted Google Puffs again?" asked Chris, before walking off to ponder Kenan's strangeness.

"Dang! It's almost been a whole day and I haven't accomplished *one* of my life's goals," Kenan lamented, as he went back behind the counter. "How am I going to do it?"

At that moment, Kel walked in, wearing an oversized jacket and a backward baseball cap, and quickly grabbed a box of dog biscuits from the shelf. "Hey, Chris! Ever eat a dog biscuit?" Kel asked jubilantly.

"No. I can't say that I have," responded Chris.

"Neither have I," said Kel, and he promptly reached into the box, pulled out a dog biscuit, and ate it, much to the disgust of Kenan and Chris. "That's darn good," Kel said with a satisfied smile.

"Great," said Chris, walking away. "Next he'll start scratching behind his ears."

"Hey," said Kel, picking up a bunch of grapes, "wanna see me put fifty grapes in my mouth? It's one of

15

my life's goals." Kel was hoping Kenan would be proud of him. "I made a whole list of stuff I wanna do. See?" With that, Kel handed Kenan a long list. While Kenan perused this list, Kel began popping the grapes into his mouth.

" 'Kel's life goals:' " read Kenan, '. . . meet an Eskimo . . . spank a walrus . . . invent a new soup . . . get rid of the rash . . .' " Kenan stopped and scolded Kel. "I thought I told you to use some ointment."

"Hamnfg ong." Kel was trying to say "hang on" as he stuffed more grapes in his mouth. His mouth, however, was only so big. Suddenly, Kel let out a loud gasp and spit out *all* the grapes—all over Kenan and all over Rigby's clean floor. Kel then took his list of goals back from Kenan and scribbled a quick change. "Let's change that to *thirty-three* grapes," he said, holding up his arms triumphantly. "I did it!"

"All you *did* was make a mess." Kenan couldn't help thinking that Kel still hadn't quite grasped the concept of life goals.

"My next goal is to read one of those magazines that women read," Kel announced. He headed over to the magazine stand and picked up a copy of *Ladies Day*. "Look at this: 'ten tips for womanly hips,' " Kel read aloud as he leafed through the magazine.

Kenan shook his head. Little did he know, but at that very moment his life was about to change. And all because of cotton balls.

"Excuse me. Do you have cotton balls?" asked a pretty young girl who had just entered the store. Kenan was mesmerized. She had big brown eyes with long eyelashes, and a long ponytail. *She looks so sweet,* he thought.

"Cot . . . cotton balls . . . yes. Yes, I do," replied Kenan nervously.

"Will you show me where to find them?" she asked. Kenan excitedly directed the pretty girl to the cotton balls and then raced over to Kel, who was still engrossed in *Ladies Day.*

"Kel!" Kenan whispered loudly. "She's here! The girl I'm going to declare my love to!" This, however, fell on deaf ears, as Kel was still heavily involved in his women's magazine.

"Did you know it only takes one week to firm your neck muscles?" Kel asked.

Kenan gave Kel a disgusted stare. "Never say that again," he warned. Kenan pointed in the direction of his new love. "Look. There she is." But when Kel started to turn around, she was looking directly toward them. Kenan quickly turned him back. "Don't look!" he instructed. "Just keep pretending to read."

"I'm not *pretending.* I know how to read!"

"Kel, just go find out her name, man!" Kenan pleaded. He turned his back to the girl, too embarrassed to look at her. "She's the beautiful girl over by the cotton balls."

"Okay . . ." But as Kel turned to look toward the cotton balls, the object of Kenan's desire had walked to another part of the store, and an old lady had taken her place by the cotton balls. Kel was shocked. *Why would*

Kenan want to go out with an old lady? he thought. "Kenan, are you sure about this?"

"Yeah!" Kenan insisted.

"She looks kind of old," Kel observed.

Kenan told Kel she was probably a senior.

"She's *definitely* a senior," Kel replied.

"Just play it cool," Kenan advised. Kel walked slowly over toward the cotton balls. Kenan, meanwhile, not wishing to appear too obvious, buried himself in the first magazine he could grab—a copy of *New Bride*. Kel approached the elderly woman.

"Excuse me, Ma'am?" he said politely.

"Yes, young man?" she responded. Kenan peeked out from behind his bride magazine, and his eyes widened with horror when he saw to whom Kel was speaking.

"Psst . . . ! No!" Kenan whispered loudly. Kel did not hear him.

"What's your name?" Kel asked the old woman.

"Not her!" Kenan now yelled loudly enough for Kel to hear him. He pointed over to the pretty girl who was in another part of the store. *"Her!"* Kenan called out.

"My name is Ethel," said the old lady.

"Oh, sorry Ma'am. We don't care," replied Kel after finally noticing the pretty girl Kenan had been pointing to. He walked briskly over to her and asked her name.

"Brianna," the girl responded, somewhat uneasily. She wasn't sure who Kel was or what he wanted.

"Her name's Brianna!" Kel screamed over to Kenan, who was so humiliated he hid behind his magazine and pretended not to hear him. "Kenan! Her name is Brianna!" Kel called out again. This time Kenan looked up and waved at her, sheepishly.

"Hi, Kenan," Brianna replied indifferently. Then she turned to Kel. "Why is he reading *New Bride* magazine?" Finally noticing the title of the magazine, Kenan nervously threw it behind him.

"Hey, Brianna?" Kel asked. "If someone was to declare their love for you, how would you want *Kenan* to do it?"

Kenan had never been more embarrassed. He forced a smile, and called out to his confused friend. "Kel? Can I see you for a moment?" Kenan then grabbed Kel and pushed him into the back room.

Kenan paced the floor of Rigby's Grocery storeroom, past the metal shelves filled with boxes, cans, and bottles. Kel sat comfortably in a small chair and watched. "Kel, is one of *your* life goals to ruin *my* life goals?" Kenan demanded.

Kel quickly looked at his list. "No, I don't see that on here," he replied.

Kenan ignored this response and told Kel about his new plan to accomplish *two* of his life goals at the same time. "See, I wanna declare my love for Brianna, right?"

"Right." Kel was paying attention. This was good.

"And I wanna climb something high like Mount Everest, right?"

"Uh-huh."

19

"Okay, follow me now," Kenan continued, "see, you and I are gonna climb to the top of the tallest building in the country—the Sears Tower."

"Hold up, Kenan. I thought you wanted us to climb to the top of Mount Everest."

"Look, Kel," explained Kenan. "Mount Everest is way too far away and too cold. The Sears Tower, meanwhile, is right here in Chicago and the stairs are indoors."

"So you're gonna declare your love to the Sears Tower? Good thinking," Kel declared.

"No! Listen, Kel . . . once we climb to the top of the Sears Tower, I can declare my love to Brianna by hanging a big ol' banner for her to see."

"How high is the Sears Tower?" Kel asked.

"One hundred and ten stories."

"Lemme know how it turns out," Kel said. He started to make his escape, but Kenan quickly grabbed him.

"You're comin' with me!"

"No!" Kel protested. "I have corns!"

Kenan dragged Kel back into the store. Chris was sweeping up Kel's spit-out grapes, and Brianna was still busy shopping. Equipped with a plan, and suddenly confident, Kenan boldly approached her.

"Brianna? Look up at the Sears Tower tonight!" instructed Kenan.

"Uh . . . Okay . . ." she responded, only because she felt some sort of response was required. She was dumbfounded. She had no idea what to make of these

two strange boys. She moved off in search of tooth-
paste.

Kenan turned to Chris and informed him of their
plans to climb to the top of the Sears Tower.

"You know, they *have* an elevator," Chris suggested.

"*Anyone* can take an elevator," scoffed Kenan. With
that, he and Kel left the store, only to return seconds
later. Now, bristling with courage, Kenan grabbed the
shocked Brianna and gave her a big kiss. Kel, feeling the
need to match Kenan's boldness, grabbed old Ethel, and
laid a big kiss right on her lips as well.

"Oh, my goodness!" Ethel exclaimed, as Kenan and
Kel finally exited Rigby's.

Kenan was out of breath as he turned the corner to
ascend another flight in the Sears Tower stairwell. He
wore a small backpack and carried a large rolled-up
banner under his arm. He stopped under a sign that
read, "30th floor" and shouted down the stairwell
behind him, "Come on Kel! You can do it!" Kel,
dressed in full mountain-climbing gear, finally turned
the corner up to the 30th floor. He struggled with his
enormous backpack.

"Are we there yet?" Kel asked, struggling to catch his
breath.

"Will you stop asking me that?" Kenan demanded.
"We still have eighty more floors to go." He then
noticed Kel was sprinkling something on the floor of the
stairwell. "What are you doing?" he asked.

"I'm leaving a trail of bread crumbs so we can find

our way back," Kel replied, wanting some credit for being so clever.

"We're just going *upstairs*," explained Kenan. "The way back is called *downstairs*. Now, come on."

So they continued their difficult climb in the name of life goals, in the name of love for Brianna, some girl who needed cotton balls.

When they reached the 73rd floor, Kel had to sit down. He was exhausted. Kenan plopped down next to him.

"Are we almost there? This is getting heavy," complained Kel, referring to his backpack.

"You shouldn't have brought so much stuff. What do you got in there?" What could Kel possibly need that would make his backpack so heavy?

"Let's see," Kel began, as he rummaged through his backpack. He pulled out some dumbbells. "Weights . . ." Kenan had difficulty understanding why Kel needed to bring weights up to the top of the Sears Tower with him.

"Hey, maybe that's what's makin' your backpack so heavy, you think?" Kenan asked sarcastically. "Did you bring any food?"

". . . dog biscuits . . ." said Kel excitedly, as he pulled out a box of dog biscuits and waved them in front of Kenan.

"Do you have any human food we can eat?" Kenan was annoyed.

Kel pulled out a huge glass bowl of fruit. "I got fruit," he offered.

"Did you have to bring the big ol' heavy bowl?" asked Kenan.

"I don't want my backpack full o' loose fruits!" exclaimed Kel, thinking this was perfectly reasonable thinking. He then reached into his backpack and pulled out a juicer. "Oh, I also brought a juicing machine to juice my fruits."

"Did it ever occur to you," said Kenan, "that carrying all this stuff might be . . . inconvenient?"

"What's your point?"

"Look, Kel, why don't we just leave this useless stuff here and pick it up on our way back? Besides, isn't that *my parents'* juicer?"

"My parents wouldn't let me bring theirs," replied Kel.

"You just keep walking," Kenan demanded, grabbing an orange from the bowl. Kel put his backpack back on, and they continued up the stairs.

By the time they reached the 109th floor, Kenan and Kel were really struggling. "One . . . more . . . floor," gasped Kenan, as he staggered to his knees.

"Man, I wish . . . I had some fresh-squeezed juice," said Kel.

Suddenly, Kenan collapsed on the ground from exhaustion. "I can't go on, Kel," he said with a sob. "Take the banner of love and go on without me. Just leave me here to die."

"Okay!" shouted Kel cheerfully, and he started up the stairs.

"Wait!" Kenan yelled. Kel stopped. Kenan struggled to catch his breath. "I'm . . . gonna . . . do it!" he insisted and began crawling bravely up the stairs.

"Hey, Kenan? What if the door to the roof is locked?" Kel asked.

Kenan stopped and stared at Kel. The thought of the door to the roof being locked had never crossed Kenan's mind. He suddenly sprang to his feet and bolted up the last flight of stairs. After a moment, Kel could hear Kenan violently yanking on a locked door.

"Noooooooooo!" Kel heard Kenan whimpering loudly.

It was sad. Kenan was so close to accomplishing two life goals: climbing to the top of something very high and declaring his love to a girl. He had the banner declaring his love to Brianna, but after climbing 110 stories, it seemed as if his chances would be dashed by one locked door. Kenan simply could not allow this to happen. He had come too far and worked too hard. He took a few steps away from the door, and using every ounce of strength left in his tired body, he threw himself up against the door once . . . twice . . . and finally, on his third attempt, he crashed the door open and triumphantly burst through onto the roof of the Sears Tower.

"I made it!" he yelled, crying tears of joy.

Kel followed Kenan and collapsed next to him.

"Now I can declare my love for Brianna," said Kenan, huffing and panting.

Kel walked over to the ledge and looked down.

"Wow! We must be fifty stories high!" exclaimed Kel, leaning dangerously far over the ledge.

Kenan quickly grabbed him and pulled him back. "It's a hundred and ten stories. Remember? That's why my feet are throbbin'."

Kel continued to peer over the edge. "Man, that's a long way down." Kel was rather observant.

Kenan glanced tentatively over the ledge. He could see all of Chicago. He could make out the Wrigley Building, Soldier Field, and the amusement park at Navy Pier, and see out to Lake Michigan. They were so high, he could swear he could almost see *Michigan* on the other end.

"Uh . . . yeah, it's a long way down," he agreed. Kenan had just remembered he was extremely afraid of heights. Especially *this* kind of heights.

Kel looked around below and noticed a window-washing scaffold. "Look, Kenan! We can just step onto this thingy right here and hang the sign real easy."

"Okay. Be careful," Kenan said nervously. They began to step off the ledge of the building. Kel reassured Kenan that this would be very easy, and, as if they were only a couple of feet off the ground, Kel jumped right onto the scaffold.

Kenan followed him very carefully into the metal basket, which hung from a giant pulley by two cables.

Kel, without a care in the world, looked down at the city below.

Kenan couldn't bring himself to look down. He simply stared at the building two feet in front of him.

"Wow, what a view!" said Kel enthusiastically. "There is no way we could be higher off the ground!"

"Nope. No way," said Kenan, still facing the wall.

"You're looking in the wrong direction, Kenan." Kel turned Kenan around, but he could barely bring himself to look. He reached down and grabbed the banner.

"Hey, whaddaya say we hang this banner and get outta here?" Kenan suggested nervously. Kel agreed and they unrolled the long banner. It read "Kenan 'Loves' Brianna," except, instead of writing the word, "loves," Kenan had drawn a giant red heart. Kel quickly taped the left side of the banner to the wall of the Sears Tower, but before Kenan could finish taping the right side, Kel was already fiddling with a control box that had been hanging from the rim of the scaffold.

"Hey," said Kel, curious about the device, "what does this thing do?"

"What's *what* do?" asked Kenan, just as he was taping the right corner of the banner to the wall. "Please don't start messin' with things—"

It was too late.

"Whooooaaa!" screamed Kenan. Kel had pressed a button, and the scaffold began moving downward. As it lowered, the right side of the banner, the part containing the last "na" of "Brianna," ripped off in Kenan's hand. The sign now read, "Kenan Loves Brian."

"We're going down!" Kenan was in a panic. "Why are we going down? Please make us stop going down."

26

"I'm trying!" shouted Kel, frantically pushing buttons. Kenan grabbed the controls from Kel, and he also began wildly pushing buttons. Suddenly, the scaffold stopped just out of reach of the roof and the sign.

"We're stuck!" cried Kenan.

"Are you sure?" asked Kel, who obviously wasn't sure.

"Of course I'm sure." "We're not moving, and 'not moving' equals 'stuck.'"

"Maybe if we rock it . . ." suggested Kel, and he began vigorously rocking the scaffold, much to the dislike and terror of Kenan.

"Don't do that! It's not helping!" Kenan protested as he quickly grabbed Kel. "Why must you be so rambunctious?" Kenan looked up at the sign, and for the first time, he noticed the accidental revision Kel caused him to make. "Aww, man! Now everybody's gonna think I love some guy named Brian!"

"You think *that's* a problem?" said Kel. "It's gonna be dark soon, and we're gonna be stuck here all night!"

"Well, don't worry," Kenan said reassuringly. "See, once we don't come home, your parents will start looking for us."

"But I told my parents that I was staying at *your* house," Kel replied.

"What?" Kenan was horrified. "My parents think I'm staying at *your* house. No one's gonna know we're missing!" With that, Kenan began to sob. Kel tried to calm him down.

"Hey, Kenan, I got an idea."

"What's your idea?" Clearly Kenan was willing to listen to anything at this point.

Kel leaned over the edge of the basket and put his idea into action. "Hellllp!" screamed Kel at the top of his lungs. "Helllp!" They were 110 stories off the ground, and no matter how loud Kel screamed, no one was going to hear them. "I give up," said Kel calmly. "Do you have a plan?"

"Well," said Kenan, "my immediate plan is to stay here all night and freeze to death."

"Well, that's not a good plan at all," replied Kel.

Kenan simply turned and glared at him.

That night a light snow began falling. Kel was at least dressed in an overcoat and wool cap, but Kenan was shivering in a bright orange T-shirt covered only by a sleeveless vest.

"Well, so far," Kenan began, "everything's going according to my plan. I'm freezing." He thought for a moment. "Wait! You got a pen?" he asked Kel. The cold wind whistled through their ears.

"Yeah . . ." Kel pulled out a pen from his backpack. "What for?"

"Look," said Kenan hopefully, "all we have to ao is write a note and throw it over. Someone on the ground will read it and rescue us."

"Well," replied Kel, "it all depends on what we write on the note. I mean, if we don't even mention that we're up here, then . . ."

"Just gimme a piece of paper!" Kenan interrupted.

He was becoming impatient with Kel. He angrily grabbed Kel's backpack and began rummaging through it, in search of a piece of paper. "Look at all this junk!" Kenan complained as he pulled out various bizarre items, one at a time. "A bowling pin . . . a cactus . . . a hair dryer . . . a *cellular phone* . . ." Kenan's eyes widened. He stared at Kel.

"What?" asked Kel defensively, as Kenan waved the cell phone in Kel's face.

"What is *this?*" asked Kenan.

"It's a cell phone. Gimme that!" Kel grabbed the phone from Kenan.

"Did you know this was in here the whole time?" asked Kenan, his voice rising.

"Yeah," replied Kel casually. "It's my mom's. But she said that I could only use it in an emergency."

Kenan held in his anger. "You wouldn't mind if I used it *anyway*, would you?" Kenan snatched the phone back from Kel and began dialing.

"Father? It's Kenan . . . your only son?" Kenan said into the phone.

Luckily, his dad remembered who Kenan was. It was late and Roger was in his bathrobe and pajamas.

"What's up?" he asked.

"Well . . . *we* are!" replied Kenan from the top of the Sears Tower. "The funniest thing happened. Hey, do you think you can pick me up?"

"Over at Kel's house?" asked Roger, still half-asleep and somewhat puzzled by the whole thing.

"Not exactly."

"You're *not* at Kel's house?" Roger was becoming angry.

"Well . . . uh . . ." Kenan peered off into the distance. "I can *see* Kel's house."

"Kenan, where are you?" Roger demanded.

"Well," replied Kenan, "do you know where the Sears Tower is? Well just go to the Sears Tower and look up. *All the way up.*"

Kel desperately grabbed the phone out of Kenan's hand. "Help, Mister Rockmore!" screamed Kel into the phone. "We're stuck! You can't miss us. We're trapped a hundred stories up, under the big sign that says 'Kenan Loves Brian'!"

Sheryl, hearing Kel's yells through the phone, rushed to put on her robe as Roger frantically dialed the phone. "Honey, what is going on? Who are you calling at this hour?"

"The fire department," Roger replied. "I've got to get Kenan and Kel down from the Sears Tower." Sheryl stopped, stunned at his reply. "Honey," Roger asked, holding the phone to his ear, "do we know a Brian?"

It was very late at night and Kenan and Kel continued to shiver on the window-washing scaffold high atop the Sears Tower.

"Kenan? How long has it been since your dad said he'd bring help?"

Kenan looked at his watch. "I don't know. My watch froze."

"Kenan? I gotta go to the bathroom," complained Kel. Kenan looked down at the faraway ground.

"Unless you can hit that tree down there, I suggest you wait," he replied.

"There's no way I can—" Suddenly, they could hear a loud whirring sound. They both looked skyward.

"Hey, look! A helicopter!" shouted Kenan, relieved.

A spotlight appeared on the two of them, as the helicopter blades blew powerful winds. The next voice they heard was on a megaphone:

"Kenan! Kel! Hang tight! We're going to drop down a ladder!" Immediately, a rope ladder dropped down to them.

"I'm goin' first!" yelled Kenan.

"I'm goin' first!" argued Kel. They continued this argument on the freezing-cold scaffold as the helicopter hovered patiently above.

"Let's flip for it," Kenan suggested.

Kel reached into his coat pocket and pulled out a quarter. "Okay," said Kel. "Heads, I go first. Tails, you go." Kel flipped the coin straight over the edge of the scaffold. They both stared down at it for what seemed like an eternity.

"Heads! I win!" shouted Kel, and he rushed to the ladder and jumped onto it.

"What?" Kenan was indignant. "Kel, you can't see a quarter from a hundred and ten stories up! Get off of that ladder!" Kenan grabbed Kel around the waist.

"Get off me, man!" yelled Kel. "You're squeezing my bladder!" Kenan refused to let go of Kel as the ladder began to ascend toward the chopper. As Kel was pulled up, his pants slid right off into Kenan's hand. Kenan stood there on the scaffold, holding Kel's pants, when he noticed he also had Kel's *underpants*. They were yellow with a smiley face on them.

"Uh oh!" exclaimed Kenan, looking up at his half-naked friend as he was being lifted up to the helicopter.

"It's freezing up heeeeeeeere!" screamed Kel.

BIG TROUBLE COMES IN SMALL BOTTLES

Kenan and Kel walk through the red curtain on the *Kenan and Kel* stage. Kel is still wearing his backpack.

"Thank you, everyone!" Kel says to the empty rows of seats. "Thank you very much."

"Kel," Kenan reminds him, "you're thanking a bunch o' chairs. This isn't our TV show, remember?"

"Oh, yeah. I forgot," says Kel.

"Hey, Kenan, do ya think the people who read this enjoyed our special adventure?"

"Of course," Kenan replies. "It was an extremely enjoyable adventure . . . as long as you weren't involved in it. But, ya know, Kel, I think we all learned something from that adventure."

Kel thinks for a moment. "That we should be patient and not try to reach all our goals all at once?"

"No. I was just kidding," Kenan chuckles. "I didn't learn a thing."

"Well, don't ya think Ernest Hemingway would've at least been proud of us?" asks Kel.

"I don't think so," replies Kenan. "We sorta' failed. I only achieved one of my three life goals."

"Well . . ." Kel has a big smile on his face, "I achieved my *biggest* life goal."

"Your biggest life goal?" Kenan says with a doubtful, wide-eyed expression. "And, what, pray tell, is that?"

"Well, Kenan, I have a little surprise."

"A surprise? What surprise?" asks Kenan. Kenan is shocked as Kel pulls out an Eskimo from behind the curtain. He wears a parka and furry, thick boots. He certainly appears to be an Eskimo.

"I got me an Eskimo!" Kel announces proudly.

"Where'd ya get 'im?" Kenan asks.

"I found 'im," brags Kel. He then turns to the dismayed Eskimo. "You're an Eskimo!" Kel announces.

"I know," replies the Eskimo.

"I can't believe you're real," says Kel as he pinches and pokes the Eskimo.

"Will you please stop that?" pleads the Eskimo. As he begins to walk away Kel follows him closely.

"But there's so many things I want to ask you. And I bet there's a lot of things you want to ask *me,*" says Kel.

The Eskimo stops and thinks about that for a second. "No. Not really," he says. Suddenly, a tall, muscular, tough-looking guy with an even tougher-looking haircut storms out onto the stage and right up to Kenan.

"Hey, are you Kenan?" he asks in a threatening tone.

"Uh, yeah. Who are you?" Kenan cringes.

"I'm Brian," replies the tough guy. "I saw your sign at the top of the Sears Tower. I didn't like it."

Kenan looks over at Kel, who shrugs. Kenan starts to stammer.

"I'm sorry. It was an accident. See what happened was we were working on setting our life goals, like Ernest Hemingway did, and I wanted to climb up something high and declare my love to a girl and . . ." Kenan stops and looks up to find that Brian is still glaring at him and doesn't seem to be enjoying the story. "Please don't hurt me," Kenan begs. Brian looks over and notices the Eskimo.

"Hey, cool Eskimo," says Brian. "Is he yours?"

"No," says Kenan, urgently. "Ya want 'im?"

"Wait a minute!" protests Kel. "*I* found that Eskimo. You can't have 'im! He was one of *my* life goals."

Kenan ignores Kel. He grabs the Eskimo by the arm and starts dragging him over to Brian.

"Here, mister Brian. He's all yours," offers Kenan.

Kel quickly grabs the Eskimo's other arm and tries to pull him back. The Eskimo becomes a human wishbone.

"Hey, wait a minute!" roars the Eskimo. "Don't I have a say in this?" He yanks himself free of Kenan and Kel and paces back and forth in a rage. "You should all be ashamed of yourselves. You can't just go around giving away Eskimos to people," he complains. Kenan, Kel, and Brian stare down at their feet.

"Ohhh, I get it," says Kel, as if he's just solved the

world's greatest mystery. "See, I think what the man is saying is, you can give out *Eskimo Pies,* but can't give out *Eskimos.*"

"Exactly!" shouts the Eskimo.

"Gee, mister Eskimo," says Brian, "I feel terrible. None of this would have happened if it weren't for that stupid sign Kenan hung up on top of the Sears Tower."

"Oh," says the Eskimo, "you mean the one that says "Kenan Loves Brian?"

"That's the one," Brian replies angrily.

"Yeah, I've seen that sign," the Eskimo said, chuckling. "You must be pretty embarrassed. You should probably get out of town for awhile until it blows over and people forget that Kenan loves you."

"I don't love him!" protests Kenan.

"Yes you do," says Kel. "It says so on the big ol' sign you hung up."

Kenan shakes his head in indescribable frustration.

"Can I go back to Alaska with you and hang out in your igloo for a few weeks until people forget?" pleads Brian to the Eskimo. The Eskimo thinks for a moment.

"I don't see why not," the Eskimo says.

"Thanks, mister Eskimo!" Brian puts his arm around the Eskimo. "You're the best Eskimo there is!"

Kenan and Kel wave good-bye as Brian and the Eskimo walk off the stage and begin their journey to Alaska. Kenan breathes a sigh of relief.

"Wow! That was close!" exclaims Kenan. "That Brian guy was pretty darn mad at me."

"And all because you loved him," replies Kel.

"I did not love him!" yells Kenan. "Would you stop sayin' that?"

"But, what's not to love about him?"

"He's not my type," replies Kenan, sarcastically.

"Do ya love *me*, Kenan? asks Kel with sad, puppy-dog eyes.

"Madly," says Kenan, rolling his eyes.

Kel seems satisfied with this response. "Well," begins Kel, "it's too bad we got into trouble again. Ya gotta admit, though, we sure created some pretty unique trouble gettin' stuck up there on that Sears Tower. I'm very proud. Not too many people can cause trouble the way you and I can."

"Not too many people can have adventures the way you and I can," adds Kenan.

"I think this calls for a celebration!" announces Kel, and he reaches into his backpack and pulls out a bottle of his all-time favorite liquid—orange soda.

Kenan observes the utter delight in Kel's face as he holds the plastic orange-soda bottle. *Let's just come right out and say it,* thinks Kenan. *Kel's love for orange soda is . . . well,* abnormal. Sure, people have their favorite foods and favorite drinks, but orange soda to Kel is the most important substance on earth. More important than water, air, or television. Kenan was convinced that if Kel ever got a cut or a scrape, his blood would be orange and carbonated.

Kel quickly opens the bottle and prepares to take a swig. "To the Earls of Adventure!" toasts Kel.

"Yep. To the Earls of Adventure," replies Kenan. Kel

throws his head back, and begins pouring the orange soda down his throat so fast, the excess liquid spills out of his mouth and onto the stage floor. Kenan watches in amazement as the entire contents of the bottle empty out.

"Look at you, spillin' orange soda all over the place, Kel. What's the matter with you?"

"I just love my orange soda!" exclaims Kel with a toothy, satisfied smile. "Who loves orange soda? *Kel* loves orange soda! Is it true? I do, I do, I do, I doooo-ooo!"

"Well, you may love your orange soda," says Kenan, "but I got a feeling, one of these days that orange soda of yours is gonna get you into some big trouble."

"Oh, come on, Kenan. How can a little ol' thing like orange soda get me into big trouble?" Kel checks his orange-soda bottle and is disappointed to find that it's empty. He immediately goes into his backpack, pulls out another one, and starts swigging it down in the same messy fashion.

"Sometimes, Kel," says Kenan in a fatherly tone, "the smallest things can lead to the biggest trouble."

Kel considers this for a moment. "I think I know what you mean, Kenan," begins Kel earnestly. "Like the time in *Andy the Anteater*—"

"Listen flapjack," Kenan interrupts. "All I'm sayin' is you might think you're all innocent and everything, drinkin' your orange soda, but I got a strong suspicion that one day—one day *soon*—that orange soda is gonna make *a lot* of people mad at you. Ooooh!"

Kenan continues. "It's gonna get you into some *big ol'* trouble!" That said, Kenan walks away, once again leaving Kel dumbfounded. Kel yells after him.

"Kenan? Kenan, whaddaya mean people are gonna be mad at me? Whaddaya mean orange soda's gonna get me into big ol' trouble? Kenan? Why do ya always call me weird nouns like 'flapjack'? Kenan? . . . Kenan?" Frustrated, Kel looks out toward the empty seats. "Aw, here it goes!" He waves his arms in disgust and follows Kenan off the stage.

"FOUL BULL"

It was another typical day at Rigby's. Shoppers shopped and Kenan sang. He was stocking cereals on the shelf, singing, *"Oh, Google Puffs, Google Puffs, the cereal that's crunchy sweet, Google Puffs, oh Google Puffs, the tasty breakfast treat!"*

All the shoppers gave him strange looks, but he continued singing. *"Oh, Google Puffs, Google Puffs—"*

Kenan abruptly halted his Google Puffs chant when he noticed a European tourist standing behind him with a video camera. "No no no, please to continue singing," said the tourist in a heavy accent from who knows where. "I am making videotape about trip to Chicago. Your singing very very bad."

Kenan was insulted. "Oh yeah? Well, your English very bad."

The tourist chuckled happily and walked away just as Chris, the store manager, arrived on the scene. "Kenan!

Careful with the cereal boxes! You're mixing up the Google Puffs with the Pood-ee-oh's!" Chris was getting worked up. The thought of mixing up the Google Puffs with the Pood-ee-oh's angered him. Chris took great pride in how organized Rigby's was.

Kenan held up the box of Pood-ee-oh's. "Ya know, why would anybody name a breakfast cereal 'Pood-ee-oh's'?"

"What's wrong with the name, 'Pood-ee-oh's'?" asked Chris in defense of the cereal.

"I don't know about you," said Kenan, "but I don't like starting off my morning with a bowl full of 'poodie.' "

Well, it wouldn't be a *truly* typical day at Rigby's without a visit from Kel, so in walked Kel at that very moment. He sneaked up behind Chris. "Boo!" Kel shouted.

"Dooh!" a startled Chris yelled as he jumped in the air. "Why'd you sneak up behind me and yell 'boo'?"

" 'Cuz I was feelin' sassy," replied Kel.

"Well go feel sassy somewhere else," demanded Chris. He was irritated because Kel was in his store again. Why was Kel always in his store? It wasn't as if Kel worked there, and he *never* bought anything. Wasn't there anywhere else he had to be? Wasn't there somewhere Kel could go? Kel walked over to the refrigerated case and pulled out a bottle of orange soda. He popped open the cap, and with great gusto, he began drinking it down as Chris raced over to him.

"Uh . . . Kel? Would you like to *pay* for that orange soda?" Chris held out his hand for some cold hard cash.

"Aw, no thanks," replied Kel. With that, he began drinking his beloved orange soda with such zeal that he was spilling as much on the floor as he was in his mouth.

Chris was appalled. "Uh . . . awwww, spilling!" shouted Chris, so upset that he had difficulty forming a sentence.

"Huh?" said Kel.

"You're spilling orange soda all over my clean floor!" He turned to Kenan. "Kenan, tell him to stop spilling orange soda all over my clean floor!"

Kenan glanced at Chris, then over at Kel. "Stop spilling orange soda all over his clean floor!" Kenan shouted, mocking Chris's exact tone and desperation.

"Kenan," said Chris, "please get a mop and clean up Kel's mess."

"My 'orangey' mess," corrected Kel.

"Yes, his 'orangey' mess," said Chris, and he shook his head and stormed off.

Kenan was annoyed. "See what you did with your orange-soda-spillin' ways? Now, I gotta clean up your—" Kenan stopped in mid-sentence and let out a brief squeal. He suddenly spotted something behind Kel that shocked and amazed him. "Rah . . ." said Kenan as if he was in a trance.

" 'Rah'?" asked Kel, puzzled at this new word.

Kenan was awestruck. He pointed to someone behind him. It was *Ron Harper,* star guard for the world champion Chicago Bulls. *Ron Harper has actually come into Rigby's.* Kenan couldn't believe it.

"Rah . . ." Kenan said again. "Ron! Ron Harper just walked in!" Kenan was finally able to get the words out.

Kel so disbelieved Kenan, he didn't even bother to turn and look. "Ron Harper? From the Chicago Bulls?" asked Kel doubtfully.

"Yeah!" insisted Kenan, pointing again. "He's right over there!"

Kel simply shook his head. "Nah-uh. You just want me to turn around so you can put a raw egg down my pants again and then break it." Kel was proud of himself. He had known Kenan for a long time, and he was on to all his tricks.

Meanwhile, Ron Harper walked near the counter where Chris was standing. "Jeepers! You're Ron Harper of the Chicago Bulls!" shouted Chris.

"Yeah, I know," replied Ron Harper. Ron Harper was no idiot. He knew who he was.

"I'm Chris," he announced proudly, and then, with a grand sweep of his hand, he bragged, "I run this whole store!"

"Congratulations," said Ron, and he shook Chris's hand.

By now, Kel had seen him, and was transformed. Kel was now a believer. "You're right, Kenan!" said Kel, pointing his finger toward the basketball player, "that *is* Ron Harper from the Chicago Bulls!"

"I told you," said Kenan. "He's comin' this way, so just be cool."

Ron walked directly over to where Kenan and Kel were standing. Kel was now out of control with excitement. "Hey, Ron! Ron Harper! I'm Kel!" he yelled.

"Kel, nice to meet you," replied Ron.

Kel was so blown away, he just stood there and laughed maniacally in Ron's face. Ron was taken aback by Kel's diabolical-sounding laughter.

"Did ya hear that, Kenan? He said it's nice to meet me! It's nice to meet *Kel!* Ron Harper said so!" Kel was losing it.

"I heard," replied Kenan, who also was very excited. "Hey, Ron," said Kenan, "you remember the time you made that free throw?"

Ron was a bit puzzled. He'd been playing basketball for many years and free throws are a common part of the game. "Which free throw are you talking about?" he asked. "I've made a lot of free throws."

Kenan laughed hysterically. "Aww, I get it! Ron made a joke. Woo hoo! That's a good one." Kenan was giddy.

Kel cut in front of Kenan, holding up his orange-soda bottle. "Hey, Ron, would you mind signin' my orange-soda bottle?" asked Kel.

"Oh, sure," said Ron obligingly. "You got a pen?"

Kel immediately began to frisk himself for a pen. Realizing he didn't have one, he frantically frisked Kenan. Kenan brushed Kel away like a bothersome mosquito.

"Stop that!" yelled Kenan.

"I'm gonna get a pen," said Kel urgently to Ron.

"Stay right here, Ron. Don't go anywhere. Stay right here." Kel raced off to find a pen.

The European tourist came racing over with his camera. "Ooooooh!" he exclaimed, with his video camera in Ron Harper's face. "It's the Ron Harper from the basketball."

Ron gave the tourist an uneasy nod. He was beginning to think that perhaps he should've gone to a different store.

Kenan approached Ron, displaying a few items from the shelves. "Say, Ron, can I help you find somethin'? Like some marshmallows? Pantyhose? Tuna?" asked a suddenly extremely helpful Kenan.

At this point, Ron was truly frightened. "No, I don't think I need any pantyhose," said Ron. "I'm just gonna browse around. Thank you." Ron started to make his way away from Kenan and down the aisle.

As Kenan watched him, he couldn't help noticing that Ron was heading straight for the large puddle of Kel's spilled orange soda. "Hey, hey Ron!" warned Kenan, "watch out for that oran—" Thud! It could be heard all through the store as Ron slipped into the air, and landed on the hard Rigby's floor.

"Ooooo! My knee!" yelled Ron Harper, who was now writhing on the floor in pain.

The European tourist had already videotaped the entire incident. "Good!" he exclaimed. "This make wonderful video!"

Chris left the counter and flew over to Ron as a

crowd gathered around him. "Mr. Harper! Are you all right?" asked the alarmed Rigby's manager. He turned to Kenan, his trusted employee. "What happened?"

An excitable woman shopper who witnessed the whole thing volunteered. "He slipped in a puddle of orange soda," explained the woman.

All the other shoppers nodded in agreement. "Orange soda," they said. "It was definitely the orange soda."

"I told you to clean up that mess!" said Chris to a bewildered Kenan.

"But, I . . . I . . ." Kenan was at a loss for words. It all happened so fast.

Meanwhile, the excitable woman shopper ran to the door and yelled out to all who could hear with one town-crier-like call: "Hey, everybody! Ron Harper slipped in a puddle of orange soda at Rigby's and got hurt reeeeeal bad!"

Suddenly a herd of people stampeded into Rigby's. Reporters, photographers, cameramen, and bystanders quickly surrounded the fallen Bulls star. Immediately they began flashing pictures and interviewing customers.

In the midst of all the commotion, Kel returned with a pen. He pushed his way through the crowd, yelling, "Ron, I got a pen!" When he finally got through, he saw Ron lying injured on the floor. "You still gonna sign my bottle?" asked Kel.

Ron just grabbed his knee and shook his head. He should never have come into Rigby's.

"I can't believe that happened," said Kenan as he and Kel walked into the Rockmores' house that evening.

"Aw, his knee didn't look all that bad," replied Kel.

"Are you kiddin'? His knee was all twisted up like a diseased pretzel! Kel, why'd you have to spill your orange soda?"

"Why didn't *you* clean it up like Chris said?" argued Kel, defensively.

This entire argument had taken place in the Rockmore living room, where Roger Rockmore was sitting on the sofa watching the evening news. "Shhhh! Keep it down," shouted Roger. "I'm trying to watch the news."

"Sorry, pop," said Kenan. He and Kel could hear the anchorman delivering the evening news:

". . . and when we come back, *bad news* for Chicago Bulls fans. A freak injury to Ron Harper in a local grocery store."

Kenan and Kel were instantly wide-eyed and terrified. Meanwhile, Roger, an avid Bulls fan, was beside himself. "Ohhh nooo!" exclaimed Roger. "The Bulls can't afford to lose Ron Harper. What could've happened to him?"

Kenan and Kel, quaking with fear, glanced at each other and shrugged. "Uhh . . . don't know," said Kenan.

"I wonder," said Kel.

"Well, I'm gonna find out," exclaimed Roger, determined to watch the rest of the news.

The commercial would be over in a matter of seconds. Kenan had to think fast. There was no way he could allow his dad to watch the rest of that news report. Roger would be upset if he figured Kenan or Kel was involved. Kenan needed to devise a quick plan. He glanced around nervously. "Uh . . . okay, mom!" yelled Kenan. "We're comin'!" He turned toward his father. "Come on, pop. Mom says dinner's ready for us in the kitchen."

Confused, Roger glanced toward the kitchen, then back at Kenan. "I didn't hear anything," he replied.

"Oh, crazy pop!" chuckled Kenan. "Always jokin' around. Now, come on, we better get in there. Dinner's ready. *In the kitchen.*" Kenan turned toward Kel and grimaced. "Right, Kel?"

"Actually," said Kel, completely confused, "I didn't hear anything eith—" Before Kel could finish, Kenan gave him a quick, hard shove. "Oooh, yeah, yeah, yeah!" said Kel, his hearing suddenly improved. "All right, Mrs. Rockmore, here we come!"

Roger shrugged. He hadn't heard his wife calling them for dinner. Maybe he needed to get his ears checked. "Okay," said Roger, getting up off the couch.

But, at that moment, as the three of them started heading toward the kitchen, the unexpected happened. Sheryl Rockmore, her arms full of groceries, walked in the front door with Kenan's little sister, Kyra. Their timing could not have been worse. "Hi, everyone," said Sheryl cheerfully.

Roger was visibly confused. Kenan was distraught. His plan had backfired and now the news was coming back on.

"I had to pick up Kyra from her karate lesson, so dinner will be a little late," said Sheryl, making her way toward the kitchen.

Roger stared peculiarly at his wife. "Okay, honey," he said. He turned to Kenan. "Son, why did you tell me your mother was in the—"

Kenan interrupted. He needed to do anything he could to get his dad's mind off that news report. "Hey, Kyra, sister," said Kenan, waving to his little sister.

Kyra was wearing her karate outfit, beaming at Kel, as was her custom. Kyra, who had had a crush on Kel for most of her young life, paid no attention to her older brother. Her mind was on Kel. "Hi, Kel," said Kyra, adoringly. Kel ignored her. More pressing matters were at hand. The news was back on.

"Shhhh!" said Roger, returning to his seat. "I want to find out what happened to Ron Harper."

Kenan stood next to his dad. He was desperate. He reached down, and nonchalantly grabbed the TV remote from the coffee table.

"Chicago Bulls star Ron Harper today," began the newsman, "slipped and fell in a puddle of—"

Bzzz! Kenan quickly changed the channel and casually looked the other way.

"Son, *what* are you doing?" asked Roger.

"I . . . I'm just tired of the news, man," said Kenan, laughing nervously. "Let's check out what Gilligan is doin'. Maybe the Professor's built a transmitter out of Mrs. Howell's hairpins."

"Kenan, give me that remote!" Roger demanded.

"I'm sorry. I can't do that, pop," responded Kenan, and he quickly tossed the remote to Kel. Roger approached Kel, and Kel immediately tossed it back to Kenan. It was a game of "keep away from Roger." The game didn't last too long, however. After only a couple more tosses, Roger grabbed Kel, placed him in a headlock, and wrested the remote away from him.

"Why'd you squeeze my head?" Kel complained.

"Hush!" Roger insisted.

That was it. Kenan had tried everything in his bag of tricks, but nothing was going to keep his dad from watching the news. He and Kel timidly walked off to the side of the room as Roger sat down and switched through the channels until he found his news program.

"Chicago Bulls star Ron Harper," continued the obliging newsman, "badly injured his knee this afternoon in a bizarre accident at a local grocery store . . ."

Roger paid close attention to the TV, as Kenan and Kel began slowly sneaking up the stairs. Suddenly, the inside of Rigby's could be seen on the TV screen. Chris was on camera, appearing shocked and bewildered.

"That's Chris!" shouted Roger. "Kenan, Kel, come here!" he demanded.

"Harper apparently slipped in a puddle of spilled orange soda . . ." continued the newsman.

"He slipped in orange soda?" said Roger, suspiciously.

"A foreign tourist was there and videotaped the entire incident . . ." the newsman continued. Roger watched a crude, shaky videotape playback of Ron Harper's accident. He cringed when he heard the loud thud of Ron hitting the floor. Kenan and Kel winced from the staircase as they played it back again and again in slow motion. "Witnesses at the scene," continued the newsman, "say the accident was the fault of these two Chicago youths . . ." Suddenly, a still shot of a smiling Kenan and Kel appeared on the TV screen.

Roger banged his feet against the floor and let out a loud, horrific yell. "Ohhhhh nooo! Noooo! No!!!" Sheryl and Kyra raced in from the kitchen.

"Roger, what is it? What's wrong?" yelled his startled wife. Roger was speechless. All he could do was point to the television screen.

"The two young men responsible for Harper's injury," continued the newsman, "have been identified as Kenan Rockmore and Kel Kimble, both local Chicago residents. As a newsman, I know I should keep my opinions to myself, but I just want to say, Kenan and Kel, we hate you!"

"I can't believe this," exclaimed Roger.

"We're going to have to move outta town!" cried Sheryl.

"It's not that bad," Kel said reassuringly.

"Yeah," said Kenan, "besides, no one really watches

the news anyway." Suddenly, a loud crash was heard, startling everyone in the room. It was the crash that a basketball makes when it's thrown through the Rockmores' living room window.

"A basketball!" yelled Kyra, rushing over to pick it up. "And there's a note on it."

"What does it say?" asked Sheryl in hysterics.

Kyra opened the note and read it aloud. "It says, 'Kenan and Kel, get out of town.'"

"Awwwww, man!" Kel whimpered.

"We're no longer popular!" cried Kenan.

The Rockmores just turned and glared at Kenan and Kel.

The next morning was by no means a typical one at Rigby's. An angry mob had gathered out in front of the store, and Chris was struggling to stack heavy boxes in front of the door to keep them out.

"We hate Rigby's! We hate Rigby's!" the crowd chanted from outside the door.

Chris placed his body in front of the door and spread his arms out wide to keep his precious store from being ransacked. "Leave me alone! Leave me be!" Chris shouted to the angry crowd. "Kenan and Kel are not here!"

At that moment, Kenan and Kel sneaked in from the back entrance. "Is the coast clear?" Kenan asked, hiding behind the cash register.

"Does it *sound* like the coast is clear?" Chris retorted. "I don't think I can hold them off much longer. It's no use. Rigby's is doomed!"

Kenan and Kel came out from behind the counter. "Have you tried calling the police?" asked Kenan.

"Most of those people out there *are* the police," replied Chris.

The angry mob's chant grew louder and louder. "We're gonna get you, Kenan and Kel! We hate Rigby's! We hate Rigby's! We're really mad at you guys!"

Kenan and Kel were scared. "Man! This is bad!" exclaimed Kenan.

"And it gets worse," said Chris. "Check out today's paper." Chris tossed the morning paper in Kenan's direction. It landed right at Kenan's feet with the front page staring him in the face. On the cover was a giant photo of Kenan and Kel wearing shocked expressions. The headline read: "BULLS SEASON IN JEOPARDY AND IT'S THEIR FAULT!"

"Aww, no! Kel, look!" said Kenan.

"I know," exclaimed Kel. "The Pope canceled his trip to Acapulco!"

Kenan grabbed the paper away from Kel and smacked him with it. "I'm not talkin' about the Pope, onion bagel! Look at this picture!"

Kel looked at the picture. "Oh. That's us," replied Kel.

"Now the whole world knows we damaged Ron Harper!" cried Kenan.

Chris put his head in his hands. He was devastated. "It's all over." He stood there in his grocer's apron and moaned. "The store, my career in groceries, gone! All gone because . . ." he pointed his finger at Kel. "Because of *you* and your orange soda!" Chris then pointed to Kenan. "And *your* inability to befollow instructions!"

" 'Befollow'?" Kenan and Kel both repeated, confused. They'd never heard *that* word before.

"Fine," said Chris, too distraught to correct his error. "Go ahead. Mock me. It doesn't matter." He moped as the angry chanting grew even louder. This was clearly the darkest moment in Chris's life. His dream of one day becoming a world famous grocer was in grave jeopardy, and it was all Kenan and Kel's fault.

Kenan sat downtrodden on his bed, holding a giant bag of hate mail, when Kel suddenly burst open his bedroom door, dressed like an outlaw from the Old West and carrying a suitcase. He was wearing a white cowboy hat and a black bandanna over his face. He was even humming cowboy-like guitar music.

"Howdy, partner," Kel greeted Kenan.

Kenan wasn't sure just what kind of rodeo was going on in Kel's head, but he was bound to find out. "Kel, why are you wearing a cowboy hat?"

"It's a disguise," replied Kel, glancing around furtively.

"Well, would you take it off!" demanded Kenan. Kenan reached up, yanked the hat off Kel's head, and gasped upon finding that Kel was now completely bald. "What happened to your hair?" screamed Kenan.

"I shaved my head so no one would recognize me,"

replied Kel, proud of this clever maneuver. Kenan simply gazed at him in wonderment.

"Uh, Kel," said Kenan, calmly, "if you were wearin' a cowboy hat as a disguise, then why would you need to shave your head, too?"

Kel thought about this and, realizing Kenan was right, began to cry.

"Aww, now don't cry," said Kenan, patting Kel on the back and carefully placing his hat back on his head. "It'll grow back."

"Okay," Kel sniffed. "I hope so." Kel then noticed the large bag of hate mail on the floor. "Hey, Kenan, what's all that?"

"Hate mail," replied Kenan. "All of Chicago hates us." Kenan then emptied the entire bag of mail onto his bed.

"Wow!" exclaimed Kel. "I betcha we're the most hated kids in Chicago!"

"Oh yeah," replied Kenan. "It's a magical day."

According to Kel, the best thing for them to do was to get out of town. And it *did* seem to make sense. After all, the entire city of Chicago wanted them out. Needless to say, Kenan and Kel were in quite a predicament.

All that notwithstanding, Kenan still refused to go. "Kel, leavin' town might be good for *us*, but what about Chris? What about our families? No, man," Kenan continued. "We caused this problem and it's up to us to fix it."

"I got an idea," said Kel. "We could sneak into the hospital and *I* could fix Ron's knee."

That, Kenan thought, *is a typical Kel statement.* "Oh, please. Kel, you can't even fix a sandwich," responded Kenan. Obviously, with no medical training whatsoever, Kel wouldn't know the first thing about fixing someone's injured knee. And how did Kel actually picture fixing Ron Harper's knee? Did he plan on using tools like a hammer and a wrench? Kenan often wondered how Kel's strange mind worked. "Besides, I have a better idea," continued Kenan. "If we can just get Ron to *forgive* us, the people of Chicago will forgive us too. That'll get us *and* Rigby's off the hook."

Kel wasn't too sure about this idea.

"Kenan and Kel . . . you bite!" yelled a heckler from outside. Kenan and Kel jumped back as a rock came crashing through Kenan's bedroom window. Kel and Kenan glanced at each other. Enough was enough.

"To the hospital?" asked Kel.

"To the hospital," replied Kenan, and they rushed out on their mission.

The elevator doors opened in the orthopedic ward of the hospital, and Kenan and Kel emerged. A quick trip into a stroage room and Kenan was cleverly disguised as a doctor. He wore a white lab coat, a stethoscope around his neck, and a fake beard and mustache. He quickly peeked out of the elevator to make sure they were on the right floor. "Fourth floor. This is it," he said, and he went back into the elevator and wheeled out Kel, who was lying on a gurney and disguised as a pregnant woman. Kel wore a long red-haired wig, bright red lipstick, and his stomach, which was stuffed with pillows to make it look as if he would give birth any minute, was easily visible in a red dress.

"Now, remember—act pregnant!" Kenan whispered to Kel.

"Right," replied Kel.

Kenan pushed him down the hallway past the nurses' station, where two nurses were discussing the injury to Ron Harper.

"I mean it," said one nurse. "If Ron Harper can't play this season, I don't know what I'll do."

"It's just a strained knee muscle," said the other nurse, trying to calm her anguished friend. "He'll be back before the playoffs. Won't he?" She began to weep. "Please say he'll be back!" she said, sobbing.

The other nurse tried to comfort her. "All I can say is those two snot-nosed kids who did this to him better leave town," she said just as Kenan and Kel were passing by.

"They're talkin' about us," whispered Kel to Kenan.

"Shhhh!" said Kenan. "Hush up."

The two nurses looked up at them strangely. "Doctor?" said one of the nurses. "You're supposed to deliver babies on the *third* floor."

Dr. Kenan had to think fast. "Uhhh . . . yes I know that . . . but uhh . . ." stammered Kenan, "there's no rooms available, so I thought I'd deliver the baby up here."

At this point, Kel figured he ought to help out. "Ohh, doctor!" yelled Kel in a high-pitched feminine voice, "The baby's a' comin'! The baby's a' comin'!"

The nurse reached down to comfort Kel. "It's all right, honey," she said, stroking Kel's hand.

"Aww, the pain!" yelled Kel in his female voice.

The other nurse appeared concerned. "Will you need some assistance, doctor?" she asked.

"No, thanks," replied Kenan. "I got it. I'll just get to the room and yank that little sucker right out." The nurses were shocked at Kenan's casual description of the impending procedure. Kenan looked down at his patient. "Let's go, Mrs. Kelly," he said, and he pushed the gurney as fast as he could. As they headed down the hallway, however, Kenan lost control. The gurney slammed right into the wall, sending Kel flying onto the floor. Kenan quickly lifted Kel up and tossed him back onto the gurney as the nurses watched in horror.

"Now what room did they say Ron was in?" whispered Kenan.

"Four-twenty-two," replied Kel.

"Four-twenty-two?" said Kenan. "That's right this way. Let's hurry." The two of them sped around the corner and down the hallway.

Kenan and Kel, still in their disguises, slowly tiptoed into room four-twenty-two. There was a man asleep on the bed, lying on his side, and facing away from them. "It looks like Ron's asleep," whispered Kel.

Kenan suggested waking him up.

"Good idea," whispered Kel. Kel glanced around and noticed a megaphone sitting on top of a cabinet for no apparent reason. He picked it up, held it to his mouth, and was about to scream into it, when Kenan grabbed it away from him.

"Put that down!" Kenan whispered loudly.

"You shouldn't yell at the pregnant," warned Kel.

Kenan was growing frustrated. "Look, we have to do this carefully," said Kenan. "We'll wake Ron up *gently,* then we'll beg for his forgiveness. Come on." They tiptoed over to the patient and lightly nudged his back. "Uhmm . . . Mr. Harper? Mr. Harper . . . ? Sir Ron . . . ?" called Kenan, quietly. There was no response whatsoever from the patient. He continued to lie perfectly still.

"Awwww!" cried Kel. "We killed Ron Harper!"

"We didn't kill 'im!" yelled Kenan.

"But he's not movin'!" shouted Kel. "Look . . ." Kel gave the patient a hard shove this time, knocking him right out of the bed, and onto the hard floor below. Kenan and Kel, as they had grown accustomed to do, winced at the loud thud. They quickly raced around to the other side of the bed to check on Ron. The patient was, in fact, very much alive, and was sitting up in a daze. Much to Kenan's surprise, however, the patient was *not* Ron Harper, but a much older man.

Kel's senses were not quite as acute. "Kenan! Ron Harper looks awful!" observed Kel.

"That's not Ron Harper," Kenan shouted, not really

understanding why Kel couldn't tell the difference. "That's a senior citizen!" Kenan was right. It was a very confused old man.

"Why'd you knock me outta my bed?" asked the old man.

Kel leaned over and whispered to Kenan, "I think we're in the wrong room."

"No kiddin', kumquat!" replied Kenan.

"I could've sworn they told me room four-twenty-four," said Kel, who was extremely perplexed and puzzled.

"You told me *four-twenty-two!*" shouted Kenan.

The old man looked up at the two weird boys and shook his head. He had no idea what was going on. "Would one of you mind helping me back into my bed?" he asked. After deciding who would take the old man's feet and who would take his head, Kenan and Kel managed to lift him up. "Careful," said the old man. "Don't bruise me."

They were just about to put him back on the bed when, suddenly, the door burst open. It was the angry Nurse Manly. She was a big, strong, mean-looking nurse. Kenan and Kel were so startled, they tossed the old man right over the other side of the bed, again sending him to the floor.

"What are you two doing in here?" demanded Nurse Manly.

Again, Kenan needed to think fast. "Uh . . . I'm Dr. . . . uh . . . Pepper . . . and . . ." Kenan pointed to

Kel, who was readjusting his wig, ". . . this is Mrs. Kelly. She's gonna have a baby."

"Ooooh! Here it comes!" screamed Kel in his female voice.

"A baby?" said Nurse Manly with a tone of emergency. "Well, let's get her on that bed and deliver that sucker!"

Kenan and Kel weren't really prepared for this. "Uh . . . okay," said Kenan. He looked over at Kel and shrugged. "Get on the bed, woman!" Kenan helped Kel lie down on the bed.

"Ooh, the pains!" yelled Kel in his high-pitched voice. "Aww, the blessed event is near!"

Nurse Manly hurried over to Kel's bedside. "Okay, Miss!" she said. "Now, listen to Nurse Manly. Start your breathing."

"Huh?" said Kel.

"Breathe!!" screamed Nurse Manly at the top of her lungs.

Kel was frightened. "Okay, okay! I'm breathin'! I'm breathin'!" cried Kel. He started breathing hard.

Nurse Manly put her hand on Kel's stomach, and was shocked at what she felt. "C'mon, doctor! Start delivering! The baby's moving!" said Nurse Manly urgently.

"Yes! Okay!" said Kenan, trying to sound professional. "Time to yank the baby!" So, Kenan had no choice. After all, he was supposed to be a doctor, and doctors know how to deliver babies. If he hadn't reached under

Kel's dress and pulled out *something*, Nurse Manly might have caught on to their masquerade. While Kel pretended to scream in pain, Kenan reached in and yanked out one of the pillows. It was a red pillow with little animals on it. Nurse Manly just stood there in shock with her mouth open. "Ahh! Well, congratulations, Mrs. Kelly!" said Kenan. "You've given birth to a fluffy baby pillow."

"Pillow? All right," said Nurse Manly, "I demand to know what happened."

Again, Kenan had to think fast. "Bug," said Kenan, pointing to Nurse Manly's face.

"Bug?" questioned Nurse Manly, nervously.

"Yeah! Bug!" exclaimed Kel.

"Bug on your forehead!" shouted Kenan, causing Nurse Manly to frantically feel her forehead.

"I don't feel anything," she said, her hand moving up and down her face.

"I'll get it!" volunteered Kenan, and he began whacking Nurse Manly in the face with the pillow. Kenan then shoved the pillow into her hands. "Take care of this baby, nurse!" instructed Kenan. "Come on, Mrs. Kelly! Time to leave." With that, he grabbed Kel and the two of them made a hasty exit from room four-twenty-two.

The old man, who had been lying on the floor all this time, finally sat up. "Ohhh!" he said, gazing at the pillow. "What a beautiful baby!"

* * *

Ron Harper was resting comfortably in his hospital bed, watching TV, when Kenan and Kel sneaked quietly into his room. They were still in their clever disguises, and at first Ron didn't recognize them.

"Hello, Ron," said Kenan. Ron looked up at them.

"Hey, what's up, Doc?" replied Ron, thinking Kenan was, in fact, a doctor.

"Uh, actually, I'm not really a doctor," admitted Kenan.

"And I'm not really a woman," admitted Kel, sadly.

Kenan then removed his fake beard and mustache, revealing his true identity. Ron recognized him immediately.

"Aw, no. Not you two!" he shouted, his voice filled with loathing and dread. Ron quickly reached for the intercom button. "Nurse! Help!" he yelled. Ron was truly scared of Kenan and Kel. They were the reason he was where he was—lying in a hospital bed.

"Now, Mr. Harper," said Kenan, "don't become all agitated."

"We just want a few minutes of your time," said Kel, humbly.

Ron put the intercom down. "Fine," said Ron, sternly. "What do you wanna say?"

Kenan and Kel could see that Ron Harper was still very angry at them for causing his accident. They felt bad for Ron, but most of all, they felt bad for themselves. They both began to cry like babies. "We're sorry!" they cried. "We're sorry we made you slip on a puddle of orange soda!" said Kenan, sobbing.

"Please forgive us!" begged Kel.

Ron was not moved. He asked Kenan and Kel to please leave him alone.

"But, Ron!" pleaded Kel. "You don't know how difficult our lives have been since the accident."

"All of Chicago hates us!" said Kenan.

"That's not my fault," said Ron. Kenan and Kel continued to plead their case to Ron, hoping that somehow they could touch his "hoops star" heart. They took turns begging.

"But you don't understand!" cried Kel.

"The police are throwing rocks through our windows!" cried Kenan.

"Our families can't go out in public!" moaned Kel.

"The store I work at is gonna have to close down!" explained Kenan.

"The Pope canceled his trip to Acapulco!" added Kel.

Ron still was not moved. "Look, fellas, why don't you two just leave me alone? Just go," ordered Ron, coldly. He repeated it again. "Just go."

Those two words pierced right through the fragile hearts of Kenan and Kel. They looked at each other, then back at Ron. "Just go?" asked Kenan.

"Just go," said Ron one more time, and Kenan and Kel filed sadly out of Ron Harper's room, weeping loudly all the way.

Just before they closed the door behind them, however, Kel popped his head back in. He had one more thing to say to Ron. "Ron? I'm sorry I made you fall," said Kel, sincerely. "And even though you won't help us, you're still my hero." With that, Kel closed the door and left.

"Hey!" someone yelled from outside Ron's room. "It's those jerks who hurt Ron Harper! Get 'em!" Ron sat up in his bed and thought about what Kel had said as he listened to the footsteps of the two boys being chased down the hallway by a violent gang of Bulls fans.

The angry mob was still out in front of Rigby's chanting their slogans of hate. "We hate Rigby's! We hate Rigby's!" they shouted. It appeared that Kenan's plan had failed, and that Kenan and Kel would, indeed, have to leave town. Kenan, Kel, and Chris sat in the empty store, moping. An elaborate barricade of shopping carts and crates had been set up carefully against the front door.

"Good-bye, Chicago," said Kenan as they contemplated their futures.

"I suppose I can always just move to another city and change my name," said Chris.

"Oooh! I always liked the name 'Bruce'!" offered Kel, not realizing that particular bit of advice was absolutely worthless.

Suddenly, something remarkable happened. The angry chanting outside Rigby's was replaced by loud cheers of joy.

"Hey! Did you hear that? What's happening?" asked Chris.

"It sounds like they're cheering," said Kenan, as the three of them rushed to the window.

"It's Ron Harper!" yelled Kel. "He's come back to hurt us!" The three of them stood behind the barricade and tried to block the door, but Ron Harper casually opened it. The door, as in all public buildings, opened from the other direction and the barricade served absolutely no purpose.

"Hello, boys," said Ron, cheerfully.

Kenan, Kel, and Chris screamed with terror, and backed away. They were certain the mighty Ron Harper had come back to Rigby's to take vengeance upon them.

"Don't be afraid," said Ron, reassuringly. Then he invited in a host of other people. A crowd of police, reporters, and cameramen filed into the store. Ron Harper had called for a press conference at Rigby's! Ron stood directly in front of a camera and began reading from a speech he had written himself. "Okay, listen up!" he shouted to the crowd. "I just want everyone to know that the injury I got here at Rigby's a few days ago was entirely *my* fault."

Kenan and Kel were frozen with shock. A collective murmur of surprise could be heard throughout the store.

"See, I was drinking some orange soda," Ron continued, "I spilled some, and *I just slipped.*"

"Yeah, yeah, that's the truth!" shouted Kel as he and Kenan walked over to Ron.

"Yeah, that's exactly what happened," explained Kenan. "Ron's a big ol' klutz!"

"So," Ron continued, briefly pausing to glare at Kenan, "Kenan and Kel didn't do anything wrong. In fact, they're good friends of mine." He put his giant NBA hands on Kenan's and Kel's shoulders, as cameras flashed all over the room.

Kenan and Kel grinned and posed for the cameras. "Yeah!" screamed Kel into the TV cameras. "Did ya hear that, Chicago?"

Ron then announced that his knee felt much better and that he'd be back on the basketball court in a week. Chris rushed over to shake Ron's hand as the crowd let out a loud cheer, and began to file out of Rigby's.

"Thanks, Mr. Harper," said Chris. "That was a wonderful thing you did. You saved my store."

"Forget that!" exclaimed Kenan. "You saved our *lives!*"

Kel, always the opportunist, reached for another bottle of orange soda, and took it over to Ron. "Hey, Ron? Will you still sign that bottle of orange soda for me?"

"Sure," replied Ron. "You got a pen?"

As Kel reached into his pocket to get a pen, he accidentally dropped the full bottle on Ron's foot. Kenan and Kel winced at the thud.

Ron yelled in pain and hobbled away from them.

TROUBLE ON THE LINE?

Kenan and Kel emerge from behind the red curtain of the stage. Kel is holding a basketball as he, once again, waves to the rows of empty seats. "Thank you! Thank you all very much!" he calls out graciously to no one.

This time, Kenan just stares at him and shakes his head. "Hey, Kel?" asks Kenan. "Did that last adventure make ya feel all happy and fuzzy?"

"It sure did," exclaims Kel. "That's what I call good adventurin'!"

"You got that right," agrees Kenan. "Didja learn what I was trying to teach you?"

"Yep," replies Kel. "The porpoise is definitely a fish and not a mammal."

"Not that!" screams Kenan. "Besides, porpoises *are* mammals, lima bean! The thing you were supposed to learn is that little things like orange soda can cause a whole lotta' trouble."

"How?" asks Kel, with a puzzled expression.

"Forget it," says Kenan, rolling his frustrated eyes to the heavens.

"Hey, Kenan, did I tell you that after the press conference, Ron showed me a few of his cool moves?"

"Really?" replies Kenan. "That's great."

"Now I can beat that old lady who lives down the street in a one-on-one."

"You mean old Mrs. Grimwilly?" asks Kenan.

"That's the one," says Kel, dribbling the ball and pretending to shoot.

"But Kel. Isn't old Mrs. Grimwilly ninety-eight years old?"

"Yeah, about that, ninety-eight, ninety-nine," replies Kel, dribbling.

"And, Kel, isn't she in a wheelchair?"

"What's your point?" asks Kel.

"No point," says Kenan. "I'm just glad you're finally good enough to beat the old woman."

"Not just Mrs. Grimwilly," Kel brags. "I'm ready to beat *anybody*." Kel dribbles the ball clumsily. It bounces off his foot and rolls away. Suddenly, three big, intimidating, athletic-looking guys walk onto the stage. One of them is holding the basketball.

"Uhm, hello," says Kenan. "What can we do for you?"

"Yeah, what's up?" asks Kel.

"*We'll* play you wimps," says the meanest-looking guy.

"Yeah," says another guy. They stare Kenan and Kel

69

down. The toughest-looking guy points to a portable basket. "We even brought our own hoop. Come on."

"Now wait," says Kenan. "There's three of you and only two of us. We should at least be allowed to pick a third player." Kenan gives Kel a sly glance and a smile.

"Fine. Get your third player," replies their menacing spokesman. "We'll still beat you badly."

"All right. Let's see, Kel . . . *whom* shall we get?" asks Kenan, with an obvious plan.

"Oh, I dunno . . ." Kel wonders out loud, "maybe . . ."

"Ro-oooon!" Kenan and Kel both yell out behind the curtain. Out walks Chicago Bulls star Ron Harper with his game face on. The three challengers suddenly look rather worried.

"Okee doke," says Kenan confidently. "Let's see. It's me . . . Kel . . . and our good friend, Chicago Bulls starting guard, Ron Harper. Why don't *we* take the ball out?" The three intimidating guys suddenly don't appear that intimidating. "Now," says Kenan smugly, as he grabs the ball from the tough guy, "I'll pass the ball to Kel . . ." Kenan casually hands the ball to Kel.

"Thank you," says Kel. "Now, I'll pass the ball to Ron . . ." Kel casually hands the ball to Ron Harper.

"Right. And I'll do this . . ." says Ron, as he powers past the stunned bullies, leaps into the air, and dunks the ball hard.

"Ooh!" shouts Kenan. "Two points for our team!"

"Um . . . we gotta go," says the tough guy, and the

three of them instantly begin pulling away their portable basketball net.

Kenan and Kel wave. "Bye, fellas!" yells Kel. "I guess *I* showed you!"

"Yeah!" shouts Kenan. "Get on outta here! And don't come back 'til ya all get game! You hear me?" Kenan then turns and shakes Ron's hand. "Thanks, Ron."

"No problem, guys. Well, I'll catch you later." With that, Ron heads back behind the curtain.

"Hey, Kenan," says Kel. "Remember that time those three big ol' mean guys challenged us to a basketball game and Chicago Bulls star Ron Harper came out from behind the curtain and saved the day?"

"Kel, what's the matter with you?" shouts Kenan. "That just happened two seconds ago, split pea!"

"Oh," says Kel. "That must be why it seems so fresh in my mind. See, Kenan," Kel begins, putting his arm around Kenan's shoulder, "you and me may get into all kinds o' trouble, and we may have really seriously dangerous Ice Capades where we get really desperate and think we're gonna die . . ."

Kenan wonders where this is going.

Kel continues. ". . . and there may be times where you and me can't stand the sight of each other and I think you're all smelly and everything, sorta like old diapers, and then you make these weird sounds in the middle of the night sometimes when you're sleepin' over that make me wanna throw up . . ."

Kenan has decided Kel is definitely rambling. When will he be finished? What could he be trying to say?

Kel continues relentlessly. ". . . and I even think there's been a couple of times when your daddy wanted to kill me but he didn't 'cuz he'd go to jail, and . . . and . . . what was I gonna say?"

"I have no idea!" shouts Kenan. "But the thing that's real important is, are ya finished?"

"Oh, wait a minute! Now I remember what I was gonna say," says Kel. "The thing I was tryin' to tell you is you and me, we have all kinds of really serious adventures, and we both like key lime pie, you see what I'm saying? And every time we eat that pie, it reminds me of the time that I upset your granddaddy so much, his spleen gave out and he had to go to the hospital . . ."

Kenan can't take it anymore. He's known Kel long enough to realize that this will never end unless he does something.

"It's just like that time in *The Pretty Little Pony*," continues Kel, "when the pretty little pony had to go to wait in line at the post office for hours and hours and . . ." As Kel continues talking, all the meaningless words blend together forming an annoying buzz-like sound. *It's like having a mosquito in your room in the middle of the night,* thinks Kenan to himself. *You just want to give it a good hard whack and stop the noise.* Kenan thinks for a moment. What could he do? Quickly, he pulls a cell phone out of his pocket and dials.

Suddenly, Kel's cell phone rings from inside his pants pocket. Kel pulls it out and answers it. "Hold on, Kenan, my phone is ringing," says Kel. "Hello?"

Kenan speaks loudly and clearly into his phone. "Kel? It's me, Kenan."

"Oh, hey, Kenan. I was just talkin' to you."

"Would you please *stop* talkin' to me, so you and me could talk on the phone?" asks Kenan.

"Okay," says Kel, "hold on." He puts the phone down, and turns and looks at Kenan. "Hey, Kenan. I gotta stop talkin' now. I got a phone call."

"That's fine," replies Kenan, who has also put his phone down. "You go ahead and take your call."

"Okay," replies Kel. He then gets back on the phone. "Kenan?" says Kel into the phone.

"This is Kenan," replies Kenan into his phone.

"Hey, Kenan. This is Kel. Why'd you call me?"

"I can't remember, but now I gotta go. I'll talk to you later."

"Okay, bye."

They both hang up their phones, and for the first time Kenan can remember, all is quiet. Kenan is proud of himself. What an ingenious means of getting Kel to quit his senseless rambling! The silence is so calming and peaceful.

Unfortunately, however, it appears too good to be true, as Kel picks his phone up again and begins dialing. "You don't mind if I make a few calls while we're standing here, do you?" asks Kel.

"But, we're in the middle of talkin' to the people, Kel."

"What people, Kenan? I forgot."

"The *readers!*" reminds Kenan loudly. *"Who* could you possibly have to call?"

"I'm a young, sociable, swingin' teenager, Kenan!" exclaims Kel. "The phone is very important to me. There's plenty of people I could call. Why do you think I carry this cell phone around with me?"

"So your momma can find you," replies Kenan.

Kel becomes irritated and defensive. "That's not true! I'm a grown boy!" Kel protests loudly. "My momma doesn't always have to know where I am. She trusts me." Kel's phone rings. "Hello? This is Kel," announces Kel proudly into his phone. ". . . oh, hi, momma . . . no, I'm here on the stage with Kenan . . ."

Kenan smiles at Kel with satisfaction.

". . . did you get the ones with the bunnies on them?" Kel continues into the phone. "Can I wear them tonight? . . . Oh, boy! Thanks momma! . . . huh?" Kel glances over at Kenan. ". . . in about two hours? . . . Okay, how about *one* hour? . . . okay, momma, I'll come home right away." Kel hangs up his phone and turns and smiles at Kenan.

"Who was that?" asks Kenan.

"Some girl," replies Kel.

"Could that girl maybe have been your . . . momma?" Kenan asks knowingly.

Kel throws his hands down and winces with disgust. "Okay, so once in a while my momma may call, but let me straighten you out right now," says Kel in an attempt to straighten Kenan out, "I got this phone because of *girls.* Girls call me every few minutes. In fact, while you and I are standing here, girls are gonna be calling me."

"All right," says Kenan. "We'll stand here for *one hour,* and I'll bet you a million dollars that not one girl calls you."

"I can't," replies Kel, sheepishly.

"Why not?" asks Kenan.

"Well, number one, my momma won't let me gamble," replies Kel. "And number 'b,' my momma says I gotta be home in *half* an hour."

Kenan rolls his eyes and shakes his head. "Look, Kel, you should be careful with that telephone anyway. It could be a dangerous thing," warns Kenan.

Kel examines the phone closely. "Why, Kenan? It doesn't have any sharp edges like scissors. I can even run with it. Look." Kel runs up and down the stage, holding his phone.

"Not dangerous *that* way, hedgehog!" shouts Kenan. "Look, Kel, all I'm tryin' to tell ya is that the telephone can get a boy into all kinds of trouble."

"It can?"

"Yep," Kenan replies. "And it can also get my daddy into all kinds o' trouble too. You'll *see.*" Kenan walks away, again leaving Kel confused and dumbfounded.

Kel calls after him. "Kenan? Kenan, whaddaya mean the phone can get a boy into all kinds of trouble? What kind of trouble? Kenan? Are we about to have another adventure? Kenan . . . !" Kel squints out at all the empty seats, and throws his hands down with disgust. "Aw, here it goes!" he says, and he runs after Kenan.

"DIAL 'O' FOR 'OOPS'"

Coffee cups clinked against saucers and cookies crunched in the Rockmore living room. Roger's incredibly nasty boss, Mr. Dawson, and his wife were over for coffee and dessert following an evening at the opera. Mr. and Mrs. Dawson sat on the couch while Sheryl Rockmore filled their cups with more coffee.

"Would you like the last piece of cake, Mrs. Dawson?" asked Roger, politely.

"You'd better take it before I do," warned Mr. Dawson.

"Oh, I feel guilty taking the last piece," Mrs. Dawson said humbly.

Being a good hostess, Sheryl insisted that Mrs. Dawson take the last piece. Just as she was about to serve it to her guest, however, Kenan and Kel burst through the front door.

"Cake!" shouted Kel, and he raced over, intercepted

the piece of cake from Sheryl, and quickly shoved it in his mouth.

Roger slapped himself in the forehead.

"Boys," said Sheryl, clearing her throat and trying to remain composed, "we have *guests.*"

"This is my son, Kenan. Son, the Dawsons took us to the opera tonight," said Roger to Kenan.

"Hey, you forgot to introduce me," said Kel, who was feeling left out.

"No, I didn't," said Roger.

Sheryl then smiled and introduced Kel to the Dawsons. "Mr. and Mrs. Dawson, this is Kenan's best friend, Kel."

"What's up?" asked Kel. That was Kel's most formal form of greeting.

"Well," said Mr. Dawson, "many airplanes are up." There was dead silence.

Kenan and Kel exchanged peculiar glances. "Huh?" they both said.

"You said, 'What's up?' " reminded Mr. Dawson. "I said, 'Many airplanes are up.' See, I work at the airport," he explained. "That's an airport joke." Happy with his explanation, the well-dressed, uptight man took a sip of his coffee surrounded by stunned reactions from the Rockmores.

Roger decided to break the tension by laughing hysterically. "A-ha-ha! Ho-ho-ho! Yah-hah! Heeeee-ooo!" laughed Roger. He had to do this. Mr. Dawson, after all, was his boss, and it was beneficial for him to laugh at his jokes, no matter how horrible they were. Sheryl and Mrs. Dawson chuckled politely.

Kenan and Kel just looked puzzled. "I don't get it," said Kel finally.

Roger cringed.

Kenan, immediately recognizing the potential embarrassment Kel could cause if he were allowed to pursue the issue, took charge of the situation. "Well, uh . . . Kel and I are gonna head upstairs," said Kenan, saving the day. "We got stuff to do."

"Nice meetin' you all," said Kel, and the two of them started up the stairs.

Much to their surprise, however, a beautiful fifteen-year-old girl in a gorgeous long black dress passed Kenan and Kel as she made her way down the stairs. Kenan was awestruck. He stopped in his tracks on the landing and gazed momentarily at the wall.

"Oh, sweetie," said Sheryl to Kenan's vision of loveliness, "did you find the restroom okay?"

"Yes, thank you," she replied.

Her voice is piped down directly from heaven, thought Kenan, as he finally made his way back down the stairs to see who this lovely person was. "Hello," said Kenan, shaking her delicate hand.

"Hi," she replied. Kenan could not stop looking into her eyes, and he could not let go of her hand.

Sheryl got up and made the introductions. "Kenan, this is Amy, Mr. and Mrs. Dawson's daughter."

"Amy," thought Kenan. Suddenly Amy was the most

important name in the world. "Amy," he repeated in his mind. Kenan's eyes widened as he continued to stare into her eyes. "Uhhh . . . nice grip," complimented Kenan.

"You too," Amy replied awkwardly.

Kenan still had not let go of her hand—another reason for Roger to cringe. "Kenan?" said Roger in a stern voice.

"Hmmm?" replied Kenan, in a daze.

"Let go," Roger instructed in a soft, pleading tone.

"Oh," said Kenan, finally realizing how weird he was being. He let go of Amy's hand. "Sorry," Kenan said.

The uptight Mr. Dawson was visibly uncomfortable with this latest development. "Well," he said, getting up off the Rockmores' sofa, "seeing that you're out of cake, I guess we should be on our way."

"Oh, won't you stay a little longer?" asked Roger out of courtesy.

"No!" shouted Mr. Dawson. It was obvious the lack of cake was not the reason he was in such a hurry to leave. Mr. Dawson didn't like the idea of Roger's lovesick son showing interest in his daughter. Mr. Dawson quickly herded his family toward the door.

"We'll walk you to your car," offered Roger.

"Whatever," replied Mr. Dawson in a haughty tone. Roger and Sheryl exited out the front door with the Dawsons.

Amy was about to follow them out, when Kenan stopped her. He had to. After all, when would he ever get to see her again? "Uhh . . . Amy?" began Kenan nervously.

"Yes?" she replied. Amy had no idea what Kenan was going to say to her, and for that matter, neither did Kenan.

And neither did Kel, watching this from the stairs.

"So . . . you all went to the opera tonight?"

"Uh-huh," replied Amy.

"Ugh!" said Kenan with a sour expression on his face. "That must have been awful!"

"No, I love the opera," she replied with a smile of sincere fondness—for the opera.

Kenan had put his foot in his mouth and needed to get it out quickly. "Ohhhh!" Kenan replied with a tone of false misunderstanding. "Me too!" Amy looked as if she didn't quite believe him. "With the people and the singin', you know," continued Kenan.

Amy was still not fooled. "Oh really?" she asked. "So, uh, what's your favorite opera?"

Kenan had to think fast. The love of his life was quizzing him on opera and if he didn't sound knowledgeable, he might lose her. "Oh, you know . . ." he said, "the one where the man is singing like . . ." Kenan began singing in a deep voice like an opera singer, much to the delight of Amy. "Lahhh—lah-lahh-lahh-lahh-lahh-lah—lahhhhh . . . !" Unfortunately for Kenan, Mr. Dawson arrived at the door in mid-"lah." ". . . hel-looooo!" sang Kenan to an impatient Mr. Dawson.

"What's the hold up?" demanded Mr. Dawson to his daughter. "Why is he bellowing?"

"Oh, Kenan was just singing me a piece from one of my favorite operas," said Amy.

Mr. Dawson was not impressed. "I don't care. Amy, your mother and I are waiting for you! Come along!"

"I'll be right there, daddy."

Mr. Dawson shot Kenan a nasty look, and walked off in a huff.

Amy turned and smiled at Kenan. If Kenan didn't know better, he might even think Amy kind of liked him. "Sorry about my dad," said Amy.

"Oh, no," replied Kenan. "He's delightful."

"Amy!" screamed Mr. Dawson from the car.

"Oooh!" exclaimed Kenan. "You better go before the man bursts into flames. You know . . ." Kenan made a loud "burst into flames" noise and waved his hands to illustrate an explosion. This was good because it got a giggle out of Amy.

"You're so funny," she said.

"Well, you know . . . I *do* enjoy the comedy," replied Kenan.

"Well . . . bye," said Amy.

It *definitely* seemed like she liked him, Kenan thought. "Bye-bye . . . farewell . . . take care now . . ." replied Kenan. He stood at the door and watched the girl of his dreams walk off into the moonlight. ". . . and remember that . . ." He turned back into the living room, and stared dreamily up at the ceiling. ". . . I love you . . ."

At that moment Roger and Sheryl walked back in.

"Aw, son," said Roger, hugging Kenan, "we love you too." Roger kissed Kenan on top of the head.

"That's sweet, boys," said Sheryl. "Well, Roger, come on, let's get this room cleaned up." Sheryl began gathering up dishes and trays.

Kenan had to find out everything he could about Amy right away. "So, uh, pop?" began Kenan. "How old is Amy?"

"Hmmm. About your age," replied Roger. "Fifteen or so." Roger began to carry a tray full of cups and saucers back into the kitchen. Kenan gently grabbed his dad's arm.

"Hmmm . . ." Kenan thought out loud. "Interesting. Uh . . . you wouldn't know, like, if she happens to have, like, a boyfriend, or a husband, or something like that?"

Roger knew exactly what his son was getting at. "Kenan," said Roger, severely, "that girl is my boss's daughter. You just stay away from her."

"But I'm a nice young man!" complained Kenan, as he followed his dad into the kitchen.

"I know that, son. It has nothing to do with you. It's her nasty father." Roger put the tray down on the counter. "Mr. Dawson is mean to everyone, and I don't want him being mean to you."

"Yeah, but pop . . ." Kenan protested.

Roger was a large, intimidating man. He stood in front of Kenan and pointed his fatherly finger at his son's chest. "You just stay away from Amy," commanded Roger.

"Yes sir," said Kenan as he moped back into the living room and picked up a fluffy pillow from a chair. He then clutched it close to his heart, as if the pillow were Amy. He hadn't yet seen Kel, who had just started back down the stairs. "Kenan and Amy Rockmore . . ." dreamt Kenan out loud as he hugged the pillow with a look of sheer bliss on his face. "Ohhhhhh . . ." Kenan then kissed the pillow.

Upon witnessing this, Kel was horrified. He put his hand over his mouth and ran quickly back up the stairs.

Kenan stood at the counter at Rigby's Grocery Store, busily scribbling into a notepad, while Kel stood nearby popping bubble wrap. Hanging out at Rigby's and popping bubble wrap was just one of the many things Kel needed to accomplish in a typical busy "Kel day." However, this time the popping sound was becoming bothersome to Kenan. "Kel, will you please stop popping those bubbles?"

"Sorry," replied Kel. "It's just that once you get started poppin', it's hard to stop."

"Well, stop!" Kenan went back to his feverish scribbling. It wasn't long before Kel resumed his loud, crackling bubble-popping. Kenan looked up angrily at Kel.

"I can't help it," said Kel, helplessly.

Chris ran in from the back room. "Do you guys hear a popping noise?" asked Chris. "It's been driving me nuts." Chris noticed Kenan completely absorbed in his writing. "What are you writing there? What is this?" he asked, grabbing Kenan's notepad away from him. After all, Chris was Kenan's boss and had a right to know what he was up to. Kenan seemed a little embarrassed as Chris scanned the notepad and read it out loud. "'Amy Amy Amy Amy Amy Amy Amy Amy Amy Amy Amy Amy Amy Amy . . .'" read Chris. "What is this?"

"It's about Amy," volunteered Kel.

"You think?" asked Chris. He began flipping through the pages of Kenan's notepad and found that all the pages were covered with the name Amy. 'Kenan, you must have written 'Amy' a thousand times! Why?"

"'Cuz I'm in love," replied Kenan dreamily.

Kel was confused. "With who?" asked Kel.

Kenan and Chris stared at Kel in disbelief of his astonishing ignorance.

"Look Kenan," said Chris, shaking his head, "if you're in love with some girl named 'Amy,' why don't you just ask her out?"

"Because I've been forbidden," replied Kenan sadly.

"By who?" asked Chris.

"His daddy!" said Kel, laughing hysterically as he grabbed a can of orange soda.

"Well," said Chris, "you should do what your father tells you."

"I agree with Chris," said Kel.

"Oh well, in that case, I must be wrong," joked Chris.

"Oh well, in that case, I must be wrong," mocked Kel in a whiny high-pitched voice.

Kenan found none of this amusing. His mind was on one thing and one thing only—Amy. "Look," said Kenan, "I'm gonna ask Amy out and that's all there is to it."

"But, Kenan," reminded Kel, "your dad said—"

"My dad is *married!*" interrupted Kenan. "He doesn't understand what it feels like to love a woman." Kenan removed his Rigby's apron and set it down on the counter. "Come along, Kel."

"Where are we going?"

"To get me a woman," Kenan boldly replied.

Chris was impressed as he watched Kenan march out of Rigby's like a man on a mission.

"Mom . . . ? Dad . . . ? Kyra . . . ?" Kenan called out as he and Kel entered his house through the front door.

"I don't think anybody's home," said Kel.

"Good," replied Kenan, rubbing his hands together like one who has devised some sort of master plan. "Now where is it?" He began searching around the living room.

"What are you looking for?" asked Kel.

"My dad's telephone book. I gotta find the Dawsons' phone number so I can call Amy."

Kel looked around and noticed the answering machine blinking. "You got messages," said Kel, helpfully.

"Just hit 'Play,'" said Kenan, continuing his thorough search of the house. Kel hit a button on the answering machine. There was a distinct rewinding noise followed by a loud beep, then there was the first message.

"Helloooo! It's grandma. Kenan, you left your teddy bear at my house, pumpkin. He misses you! Come visit Grammy! I'll give your teddy bear a kiss." Then came the kissing noises.

Kenan stared at Kel as if to say, "Don't even think of saying what you're about to say."

Kel couldn't help himself. "Awwww! Your teddy bear misses you," mocked Kel.

"You're about to be missing some *teeth,"* replied Kenan, shaking his fist at Kel.

There was another loud beep. This time it was a message from Roger. Kenan and Kel listened while they searched: "Honey, this is Roger. Mr. Dawson says I gotta work late again!" he complained. "I'll tell you what, that Dawson is a nasty, evil, bull-headed, unreasonable jerk! Oh well . . . I better get back to work before the *idiot* comes back. Bye-bye, sweetheart." That was the last message on the machine.

"Ooh!" exclaimed Kel. "He *does* sound mean. You better leave Mister Dawson's daughter alone!"

Though it did sound like Mr. Dawson was an awful, difficult man, Kenan paid no attention to Kel's advice and reached into his dad's desk. "Ah hah!" yelled Kenan triumphantly. "Here's my dad's address book." He displayed it proudly, then began rifling through the pages. "Let's see . . . Daffle . . . Dagman . . . Dawson! Here it is!'' Kenan quickly wrote down the information. "C'mon, Kel.'' Kenan and Kel then raced upstairs to make the most important call of Kenan's young life.

Kel stood in Kenan's room and watched as Kenan sat on his bed, holding the phone. He picked it up, then he put it back down. He picked it up again, started to dial, then put it back down.

"What are you doing?'' asked Kel.

"I'm not ready to call her yet,'' explained Kenan. "I need to practice.'' He put the phone down and picked up a shoe from the floor. "Here,'' said Kenan, tossing the shoe to Kel. "You be Amy.''

Kel was delighted. Most guys would hate the idea of having to pretend to be a girl, but not Kel. "Okay,'' said Kel. "Who are *you* gonna be?''

Kenan glared at Kel with one eye closed, as if to try to get a better look at Kel—perhaps to see if he really could be *that* ignorant. "Me!'' shouted Kenan. "I'll be *me!*''

"Okay, cool,'' replied Kel.

Kenan picked up the phone and pretended to dial while Kel practiced being Amy Dawson. He fluttered his arms and pranced about as if he were a girl playing hard to get.

"Ring!'' said Kenan, imitating a ringing phone. "Ring! . . . Ring!'' Kenan said again. Kel was not answering his shoe. Instead, he was standing in front of the mirror pretending to put on lipstick. Kenan had that wide-eyed expression of dismay which indicated he was becoming extremely irritated. "Man, pick up the shoe!" screamed Kenan, completely out of patience.

"Okay," replied Kel, and he rushed over to answer the shoe. "Hellloooo?" said Kel, in a phony high-pitched feminine voice. He even tucked his free hand under his elbow like he thought girls so often do.

"Yes, is this Amy?" said Kenan into the phone. He was taking this quite seriously.

"Why, yes it is," replied Kel in his girlish voice.

"Hi, this is Kenan."

"Oh, Kenan!" said Kel, pretending to be an excited Amy Dawson. "Hold on. Let me get off the other shoe." Kel pretended to press a button on the shoe, as if there was someone holding on another line. "Girl!" he screamed. "Guess who I got on the other line? It's Kenan! You know. The one with the little dreadlocks and stuff?" He fanned himself, pretending to be overcome with excitement. "I gotta call you back!" He pressed the imaginary button again, made himself comfortable on Kenan's desk (crossing one leg over the other), regained his composure, and resumed his shoe conversation with Kenan. "Okay, I'm back," he said coyly, in his female voice.

Stunned, Kenan momentarily stared at Kel before continuing his practice call. "Yeah, uh, Amy . . . would you like to go out with me sometime?"

"Uh . . . no," replied Kel as Amy.

Kenan was becoming annoyed again. "C'mon, man!" he yelled. Kenan was still nervous even though he was really just asking Kel for a date.

"Sorry," said Kel in his normal voice. He spoke into the shoe again in his girl voice. "Oh sure, Kenan. I'd love to go out with you!"

"Great," Kenan replied. "Uh, so maybe we'll, like, go to a movie or something?"

Kel giggled. "Oh, Kenan! You animal!"

"Uh . . . well, I guess it's a date." said Kenan.

"Ooh!" exclaimed Kel as Amy. "I can't wait. I'm gonna dress all pretty, and I'm gonna wear a pretty dress and . . ."

At that point, Kenan had enough. "Stop it, man! Just hang up the shoe!" yelled Kenan.

"I think you're ready," said Kel.

"You're ready for a *psychiatrist,"* replied Kenan. Kenan did feel like he was ready, however, and he picked up the phone and dialed Amy's number—*for real.*

"It's ringing," said Kenan nervously, with his ear to the phone.

The phone rang four times before the Dawsons' answering machine picked up. It was Mr. Dawson's mean, nasty voice on the machine. It sounded as if he were bawling people out for calling their house. "This is the Dawsons' residence. No one is here to take your call. Leave your name and number at the beep tone. We'll call you back when we have time!" said the stern announcement on the Dawsons' machine.

Kenan was in a panic. He put his hand over the mouthpiece and looked at Kel. "It's their answering machine. What should I do?'' Kenan fumbled with the phone receiver before finally handing it to Kel.

Kel shoved it right back into Kenan's hands, and Kenan gave it right back to Kel. "I don't want it!" said Kel, and he hastily put down the receiver. "Why didn't you just leave a message?"

"I didn't practice leaving a message," replied Kenan, somewhat flustered by the whole experience.

"Well, I think you're better off," said Kel. "I don't see why you wanna date a girl whose father is a mean, horrible jerk."

"My *father's* the one who thinks Mister Dawson's a mean horrible jerk," Kenan explained. "One time, my dad said Mr. Dawson was so dumb, he couldn't find his own face with both hands!" Kenan and Kel had a good laugh.

"Man, how can your daddy work for a man who's so mean *and* dumb?" asked Kel, chuckling.

"Oh, man!" exclaimed Kenan. "Pop says he's gonna have Mr. Dawson's job before too long. See, he's just waiting 'til the jerk—" Kenan suddenly stopped cold in mid-sentence. He spotted something very disturbing. Struck with horror, he put his hand over his mouth. He stared at the telephone, then let out a loud, high-pitched squeal.

"What? Kenan, what's wrong?" asked Kel. "Kenan?"

"Stop saying my name!" cried Kenan desperately.

"Why, Kenan?" asked Kel, confused.

Kenan pointed to the phone. It was sitting way off the hook. How could Kel have thought it was hung up? It wasn't even *close* to being hung up. "The . . . the phone!" whispered Kenan in a panic. "You didn't hang up the *phone!*"

"So?" Kel whispered back.

"So," said Kenan, in a shaky, terrified voice, *"everything we just said was being recorded on the Dawsons' answering machine!"*

This time both Kenan *and* Kel let out high-pitched squeals of alarm and dread.

With nothing left to do, Kenan picked up the receiver and began to whimper into it. "I'm sorrryyyy . . . Ohhh, forgive me! . . ." cried Kenan into the phone. "Please don't fire my daddy! . . . I didn't mean to . . . uhm . . . this isn't even Kenan! . . . It's uh . . ." Kenan thought fast. He quickly adopted a Spanish accent, ". . . it's Fernando! Fernando Montalban! I don't even know nobody named Kenan . . . uhm . . . ohhh . . ." Kenan slowly hung up the phone and put his head in his hands.

I am in serious trouble.

All he had wanted to do was talk to Amy, the love of his life, and now his dad's job was in jeopardy.

"Smooooth," said Kel.

Kenan frantically raced down the stairs into the living room and was headed toward the front door.

Kel followed close behind. "Kenan? Kenan, where are you goin'?"

"We gotta stop the Dawsons from hearing that phone message!" shouted Kenan in a frenzy.

"How're you gonna do that?" asked Kel.

Kenan opened the door, then closed it, then paced aimlessly around the room. "I don't know," he whined.

Suddenly Kel saw Kenan's finger point into the air. It was Kenan's "idea finger." Kel cringed and covered his ears when Kenan said, "Wait! I got an idea!" He didn't want to hear it. He'd heard enough of Kenan's ideas, and they always resulted in disaster. *Why,* thought Kel, *must Kenan keep having ideas?*

Kenan chased Kel around the living room with his idea, then finally caught him and pried Kel's hands away from his ears. "All we gotta do," began Kenan with a tone of utter simplicity, "is get in their house and replace their answering machine tape with a new one."

"Well, good luck," said Kel, giving Kenan a friendly pat on the back. "Let me know how it turns out." With that, Kel made his way toward the door.

Kenan quickly grabbed Kel by the hood of his sweatshirt. "You're gonna know how it turns out because you're gonna help me!" said Kenan, bringing Kel back into the living room.

"Awww, I knew I would end up in a predicament!" moaned Kel.

"I promise nothing bad's gonna happen," said Kenan reassuringly.

Kel was as scared as a three-year-old about to go on his first roller-coaster ride. He whined and wailed. "Awwwww . . ." moaned Kel again.

"Kel, we don't have time for you to say, 'Awwwww,'" scolded Kenan. "Now listen: you get a fresh answering machine tape and then meet me at Amy's house." He handed Kel the address. "I gotta get over there before the Dawsons get home. Hurry up!" Kenan then raced out the front door.

Kel called out after him. "But, Kenan . . . ? Where am I gonna find a fresh answering-machine tape? Kenan? Where am I gonna . . . oh, I'm talking to myself," concluded Kel, as he grudgingly began his search.

All was quiet in front of the Dawsons' house that evening, as Kenan tiptoed onto their porch. He was peering through their large picture window, struggling to see through the closed curtains.

Little did Kenan know that Kel had just arrived and was standing right behind him, chewing a giant wad of gum. "They're not home?" asked Kel, at what seemed like the top of his lungs. Kenan jumped a few feet in the air, screamed, then assumed a karate stance before finally realizing it was only Kel.

"You scared me!" Kenan shouted.

"You scared *me!*" replied Kel.

"Did you bring the tape?" asked Kenan through clenched-teeth.

Kel proudly removed an answering-machine tape from the pocket of his overalls and displayed it to Kenan.

"Good." said Kenan. "Nobody's home."

"Are you sure?" asked Kel, glancing around nervously.

"I think so," replied Kenan. He looked around and noticed a window above the front door. "Look through that window up there. You'll get a better view of the inside of their house." Kenan cupped his hands to give Kel a boost, and Kel began his difficult climb up Kenan. He put one foot in Kenan's hands, grabbed onto Kenan's shoulders, and almost made it to the window. "See anything?" asked Kenan, who was holding Kel's legs while struggling to keep his balance.

"Hang on," replied Kel. Kel grabbed on to the porch light to hold himself up, but it gave way. Kenan and Kel came tumbling to the ground, Kel landing right on top of Kenan.

"Get off me!" yelled Kenan, sprawled out on the Dawsons' porch. It wasn't until they got to their feet that Kenan noticed the porch light dangling from a wire in the wall.

"Don't worry. I can fix that," offered Kel. But no sooner did Kel touch it than the light came crashing to the ground and broke into several pieces. "I can't fix *that*," whined Kel.

Kenan was beside himself. "Oooh! Why'd you have to rip the porch light outta the wall?!"

While Kel was apologizing for breaking the light, Kenan noticed the mail slot at the bottom of the Dawsons' front door. He got down on his knees, opened the slot, and peered through into the Dawsons' living room. "Hey!" Kenan whispered loudly. "I can see their answering machine! It's blinking! That means they haven't listened to the message yet!" Sure enough, there it was, sitting on a table next to a lamp and blinking wildly for all to see. Kenan's future and, more importantly, his dad's future were somewhere in that answering machine.

"Let me see," said Kel. He reached his hand through the mail slot to hold it open. "I see it!" exclaimed Kel. Suddenly, the boys could hear something dropping on the floor just inside the Dawsons' front door.

"What was that?" asked Kenan.

"My watch fell off," replied Kel.

"Awww! We can't let the Dawsons find your watch!"

"I can get it," said Kel. "I'll put my gum on the end of a stick or something and fish it out."

"Okay, but this better work," cautioned Kenan.

Kel started looking around the Dawsons' porch for something long and narrow. His eyes rested on the garden hose. It had a tapered nozzle that he thought would do the trick. "Perfect!" exclaimed Kel. "We can put the gum on the end of this nozzle." Kel picked up the hose and took it over to the front door. He then stopped to chew his gum vigorously. This was important, because if the gum were not thoroughly chewed, it might not have the stickiness necessary to hold on to something as heavy as a watch.

Kenan was becoming nervous and impatient. "Just hurry up!" shouted Kenan.

So, Kel placed the gum at the tip of the nozzle, then carefully stuck the hose down the Dawsons' mail slot.

To add to the excitement of the moment, Kel provided his own action music. "Dee dee dee dee-dee, dee dee dee dee-dee," sang Kel, as they tried to guide the hose through the mail slot toward Kel's watch, which lay on the Dawsons' living-room floor. "There . . . I almost got it . . ." said Kel.

Then they heard another light "plop!" It was the sound of Kel's gum falling off the hose nozzle.

"Gimme that nozzle!" demanded Kenan, taking the hose away from Kel. "I just gotta stretch the hose a little bit . . ." Kenan gave the hose a yank. "It's stuck or somethin', Kel. Help me yank the hose." Kenan and Kel both pulled hard on the hose. Little did they realize that the hose was caught around the knob on the porch that turned the water on. The harder they yanked, the more the knob turned. Suddenly, the distinct sound of water traveling through a hose could be heard. "What's that noise?" asked Kenan.

"I don't know," replied Kel.

"Something's going on in there!" said Kenan, pressing his ear to the door. He quickly leaned down, gazed into the mail slot, and emitted a loud, shrill scream.

"What?" asked Kel.

"The hose! The hose is on!" shouted Kenan. Water was shooting out of the nozzle, directly into the Dawsons' living room. Kenan screamed. He tried to pull the hose out of the mail slot, but it became stuck and wouldn't budge. "Turn it off! Turn off the water!" shouted Kenan as he tried to maneuver the hose out of the slot. It was too late. He lost all control of the hose.

It seemed to have a mind of its own, as it flailed all over the place, spraying water throughout the Dawsons' living room. Kel raced over to the spigot and turned it frantically, but he was turning it the wrong way. The water pressure grew stronger. Statuettes were sprayed off shelves, an oil painting was ruined, lamps were knocked down, and the furniture was completely soaked. "Turn off the water!" yelled Kenan again.

Kel continued turning the spigot until, finally, it came off in his hand. *Yikes!* "Kenan . . . ?"

"Turn off the water!" yelled Kenan, too busy struggling with the hose to even look at Kel.

"Kenan . . . ?"

"Turn off the water!" screamed Kenan, still not looking.

"Kenan . . . ?" said Kel again, this time tapping him on the shoulder.

When Kenan turned to see Kel holding the broken knob in his hand, his face completely changed shape. He let out a blood-curdling shriek.

"Now what do we do?" cried Kel as the water continued to pour into the Dawsons' house faster than ever.

Kenan glanced around desperately. "Grab those hedge clippers!" he yelled. Kel promptly picked up a large pair of hedge clippers and cut the hose in half.

"Now get it outta here!" screamed Kenan, and Kel ran off with the spewing end of the hose, but the damage had already been done. Through the mail slot, Kenan could see the Dawsons' living room had been destroyed by the out-of-control hose. Kenan finally managed to pull the remaining piece of the hose out of the mail slot. "Punk!" he yelled at the piece of hose, then angrily tossed it aside.

"Owww!" screamed Kel, having just been accidentally nailed in the head by a piece of hose thrown by his best friend. "Why'd ya fling that piece of hose at me?"

Kenan felt terrible. He gave Kel an apologetic hug. *It's all my own fault,* thought Kenan. If he could only have controlled his feelings for Amy, the Dawsons would still have a dry living room, his dad would still have a job to report to on Monday, and Kel wouldn't have been hit in the head with a garden hose.

"I'm sorry," said Kenan. "Are you okay?"

Kel nodded his head slowly. They both bent down and peered one more time through the mail slot.

"Ohhhh . . ." whimpered Kenan, as they surveyed the damage. "Soaking . . . soaking wet . . . couch . . . chairs . . . draperies . . . oh, the moisture! It's just wrong! Everything's all wrong!" They both collapsed in a heap on the porch with their backs against the door.

"I got an idea," said Kel.

"What?" asked Kenan, willing to listen to anything. Even an idea of Kel's.

"Let's run away!"

"We can't run away," replied Kenan. Kel couldn't understand why not. It seemed like a perfectly reasonable solution after destroying so many lives and so much property in so little time. "We're not leavin'!" said Kenan, boldly. "We're gonna sit right here 'til the

Dawsons get home so we can switch that tape." It had been a long day and they were both exhausted. Kenan put his head on Kel's shoulder and they both fell asleep right there against the Dawsons' front door.

It was a bright and sunny morning. The birds were chirping loudly, and the morning paper landed right smack in Kenan's face, jarring him awake. He looked around and slowly remembered where he was. "Wake up, Kel," said Kenan, nudging him. "We've been out here all night!"

The Dawsons had only just arrived home entering through the back door after having spent the night with Amy's grandmother. They carried small suitcases from the garage through the kitchen into the living room. "I sure wish we could have stayed longer," said Mr. Dawson.

"One night at your mother's house is enough," replied Mrs. Dawson.

"I like seeing grandma," said Amy. Then, they suddenly noticed the mess in their house. Not unlike the three bears, they scanned the living room with stunned expressions.

"What in the world?" exclaimed Mr. Dawson.

"My goodness! Everything is soaking wet!" shrieked Mrs. Dawson.

"What happened?" asked Amy. They were all rather confused as they looked around the wet room.

"Where did all this water come from?" asked Mrs. Dawson.

"A pipe must have burst," said her husband for lack of a better explanation. Mr. Dawson noticed the mail sitting on the floor right below the mail slot. He bent down to pick it up. "Oh, no! The mail's all wet, too."

Then, he saw it.

A watch was sitting there on the floor as plain as day.

"Whose watch is this?" he bellowed.

Kenan and Kel sat on the Dawsons' porch, trying to wake up. "Our parents are gonna kill us," said Kel, his sleepy eyes still adjusting to the sunlight. "What time is it?" Kel looked at his wrist and remembered his watch was still in the Dawsons' living room. "Uh-oh, what about my watch?"

"Your watch is the *last* thing I'm worried about," said Kenan.

"But I want my watch," Kel protested.

"Maybe I can reach it with my arm," said Kenan. "Can you believe the Dawsons haven't come home yet?" he asked as he turned toward the door, rolled up his sleeve, and reached his arm through the mail slot.

"What the . . . ? What *is* that?" Kenan had a puzzled expression as he tried to figure out what it was he was touching through the mail slot.

Meanwhile Kel noticed something strange in the driveway. *Hmm . . .* he thought. He tapped Kenan on the back. "Hey, Kenan? Was that car in the driveway last night?" asked Kel, pointing to the Dawsons' driveway.

"No," said Kenan. Suddenly, Kenan's expression turned to one of shock and horror.

In the Dawson living room, Mr. Dawson stared down at Kenan's hand as it grabbed his knee through the mail slot. When Mr. Dawson finally swung open the door, Kenan, his arm still in the slot, slid right into the Dawson living room.

"Heyyyy, what's going on, ya all?" said Kenan, looking up from his knees at Mr. Dawson. "Remember me?" If this wasn't the absolute most embarrassing moment in Kenan Rockmore's life, it had to be awfully high on the list.

"Kenan?" said Amy, somewhat surprised to see him on their living room floor with his arm through their mail slot.

Kenan waved to her with his one free hand. "Hey, Amy. Nice to see you."

Mr. Dawson was always angry, but this time, he was *really* angry. "What are you doing here?" he demanded.

"Mind if I come in?" asked Kenan politely.

"You *are* in!" shouted Mr. Dawson.

Kenan finally managed to remove his arm from the mail slot and he walked into the wet living room with Kel right behind him. "You all remember my friend, Kel?" asked Kenan.

"Got yer paper," said Kel as he handed Mr. Dawson his morning paper, then sat right down on the Dawsons' couch. "Eeooh!" yelled Kel, jumping up. "Your couch is wet!"

Kenan slapped Kel in the head.

Mr. Dawson glared at them. "Young man?! What is the meaning of this?" he screamed.

Kenan stared at the blinking answering machine and motioned to Kel, who nodded and made his way over to the machine. Now all Kenan had to do was distract the Dawsons while Kel switched the answering-machine tapes.

"Meaning of what, sir?" asked Kenan timidly.

"The meaning," Mr. Dawson roared, "of your arm sticking through the front door and . . . *grabbing me!*"

"Oh, it's funny really . . ." said Kenan, who had no idea what he was going to say.

Mr. Dawson approached Kenan and put his face right up against Kenan's face in a rather intimidating fashion. "Well, then . . ." Mr. Dawson said sternly, *"make me laugh."*

Kenan chuckled nervously. "Heh heh . . . oh, you're all going to laugh," said Kenan. "Laaaaaugh and laaauughh!"

"Kenan, what's going on?" asked Amy.

"Well, I'm gonna get to that part," said Kenan. "Why don't you all come in and have a seat? Of course you'll all have to sit on the table 'cuz everything is wet."

Amy and Mrs. Dawson sat down on the coffee table to hear Kenan's explanation. Mr. Dawson chose to stand with his arms folded in an angry, threatening manner. Meanwhile, Kel was busily at work over by the answering machine attempting to remove the Dawsons' tape.

"Well, it all started a long time ago . . ." began Kenan, ". . . when I was just a little thing . . . uh . . . little Kenan is what they called me . . . see . . . 'cuz I was smaller than I am now . . ." Kenan didn't care that his story made no sense, as long as it kept the Dawsons occupied long enough for Kel to switch the tapes. Behind the Dawsons, out of the corner of his eye, Kenan could see Kel struggling furiously with the tiny tape. He unraveled it, and at one point was completely tangled in it. He reached into a drawer, found a scissors, and cut himself free.

". . . I mean at four years old . . ." Kenan continued his desperate rambling, ". . . one is hardly big . . . heh heh . . . so, anyhow . . . uh, like I was saying . . . my daddy loves you, Mister Dawson . . . so anyway, one day . . . oh, I'll never forget the day . . . see this is the funny part right here . . ."

"Oh yeah?" said Mr. Dawson. "I was wondering when I was going to go 'ha-ha.'"

"Soon. Real soon," said Kenan. "See, it was a dark and stormy night . . . or day, whichever you all prefer . . ." Kenan noticed that Kel had accidentally roped himself around the neck with tape and pulled himself to the ground. "See, it was a stormy evening . . ." continued Kenan, ". . . and that's when I came to be . . ."

"Done!" yelled Kel triumphantly, smiling ear to ear.

"And that's my story!" Kenan chuckled, his story suddenly finished.

"We heard *no* story," said a confused Mrs. Dawson.

Kenan snapped his finger and pointed at her. "You know, you're right. I gotta work on coming up with a better story. Come along, Kel!" he said, and he and Kel began to back their way toward the door.

"Nice seeing you all!" said Kel.

"All righty," said Kenan. "Now if we could all just forget this whole thing *ever* happened . . ."

They turned to leave. They were only a few feet away from freedom when Mr. Dawson bellowed, "Hold it!" Kenan and Kel froze in their tracks and squealed with dread. Mr. Dawson was not a man who could be easily fooled. "I don't know what's going on here," he said, "but I'm going to get your father on the phone."

"Aw, you don't wanna do that," Kenan pleaded. "Y'all take care, now." Kenan and Kel made their way toward the door again.

"Stay where you are!" shouted Mr. Dawson. He was a scary man. He walked deliberately over to the phone, lifted the receiver, and was just about to call Mr. Rockmore when Kel saved the day . . . sort of.

"Oh, you can play your messages now if you want," Kel offered.

"Thank you very much," replied Mr. Dawson, menacingly. Mr. Dawson leaned over and pressed the "Play" button on his answering machine. A loud beep could be heard, followed by the message from Kenan's grandmother they had heard earlier: "Helloooo! It's grandma. Kenan, you left your teddy bear at my house, pumpkin . . ."

Kenan was horrified.

"What is *your* grandma doing calling *our* machine?" demanded Mr. Dawson.

"He misses you!" continued the message. "Come visit Grammy! I'll give your teddy bear a kiss."

Kenan spun Kel around. "What tape did you put in the machine?" whispered Kenan.

"I took the tape out of the machine at *your* house," Kel replied timidly.

Kenan did a frustrated double arm swing. "Whyyyyyyyy?!" Kenan moaned.

The Dawsons stood in their wet living room, their arms folded and their faces squinting with confusion as their machine beeped a second time.

"Honey, this is Roger," began the next message.

"That's your father!" said Mr. Dawson, pointing to Kenan.

Kenan let out the high-pitched squeal of a frightened mouse. They all listened in silence as the sound of Roger's voice rang out on the Dawsons' answering machine: ". . . Mister Dawson says I gotta work late again!" Roger complained. "I'll tell you what, that Dawson is a nasty, evil, bull-headed, unreasonable jerk! Oh well . . . I better get back to work before the *idiot* comes back. Bye-bye, sweetheart."

The Dawsons stared angrily at Kenan and Kel. Kel

whimpered and hid behind Kenan, who looked coyly at Amy.

"So . . . uh . . . Amy . . . ?" asked Kenan, with nothing left to lose. "Maybe I can call you again later, you know, after your house dries up?"

The Dawsons just stood and stared at the two strange boys in their soaking wet living room.

NOW, THOSE WERE SOME *SERIOUS* ADVENTURES!

Kenan and Kel make their way through the red curtain on the stage. Kel acknowledges the room full of empty chairs. "Thank you, everybody! Oh, yeah! Woo hoo! Thank ya, thank ya, thank ya!"

"Will you cut that out?" yells Kenan, slapping him lightly on the back of the head.

"Oh, I get it," complains Kel. "It's 'Abuse the Kel' Day. First it was that nasty piece of garden hose, now you're slappin' me on the head."

"I'm sorrrry," says Kenan, feeling truly sorry. He gives Kel a big hug. "It's just that I can't seem to get you to understand that this wasn't our television program and that there's *no one* out there." Kenan points out to the empty rows of chairs.

"So, let me get this straight," says Kel. "You and I aren't talkin' to the audience 'cuz there is no audience."

"Right," says Kenan. "You're gettin' it just in time for the last couple of pages."

"So, you and me," Kel continues, "we're in a book?"

"Now, you're *really* gettin' it," says Kenan.

"And the people . . ." Kel thinks out loud, with his hand on his chin, ". . . they read what you and me are sayin'?"

"Preeee-cisely!" shouts Kenan.

"I'm confused," says Kel. "Oh, well. I guess that's why I'm the Princess of Confusion."

"I guess so," says Kenan.

"So, what did you think of that last adventure?" asks Kenan.

"That was some nasty adventuring!" exclaims Kel. "Trouble like that don't grow on trees. Yep!" continues Kel, as if he were extremely proud of himself. "You and me are to trouble what Michael Jordan is to basketball."

"Yeah." Kenan thinks for a minute. "But, see, Kel, isn't the whole thing about Michael Jordan that he *tries* to be good on the basketball court?"

"Are you kidding?" laughs Kel. "The way he shoots and flies around and dribbles and scores and all that kinda stuff . . . he doesn't do it by accident!"

"But, see Kenan, all that trouble we just got into . . . that *was* by accident."

"Huh?" says Kel.

"Think about it," says Kenan. "The trouble only happened 'cause you *accidentally* forgot to hang up the phone all the way. Remember?"

"So, what you're saying is, we're a couple of fools, and we're really not that good at anything?"

"Yeah, I guess that is what I'm saying," says Kenan,

putting a consoling arm around Kel. "But we're still the Earls of Adventure."

"Yeah, we're still the Earls of Adventure!" shouts Kel.

"We sure are," agrees Kenan, as they high five each other.

"So, whatever happened with your daddy?" asks Kel. "Did he get fired?"

"Nah," says Kenan. "I think he was *gonna* get fired, but, luckily, that mean old Mr. Dawson got transferred to Alaska before he could get the chance."

"My, how convenient," says Kel.

"Isn't it?" says Kenan with a big smile. Suddenly, much to Kenan's delight, the lovely Amy emerges through the curtain.

"Hi, Kenan," says Amy.

"Amy?" says Kenan, his palms already sweaty and his heart beating a mile a minute. "I never thought I'd see you again. What's up?"

"Well, Kenan, you asked me out, and I just wanted to tell you that I would *love* to go out with you."

"Well, alllll right!" shouts Kenan, and he begins doing a little dance around the stage. Kel, happy for his friend, joins in. The two of them dance a circle around Amy.

She's becoming dizzy watching them. "But, I can't," says Amy, sadly.

Immediately Kenan's eyes widen and he stops dancing. Kel, however, doesn't quite get it. He continues his dance of celebration until Kenan finally walks over and taps him on the back. "Man, would you stop dancin?" yells Kenan. "She said 'can't.'"

Kel stops dancing. "She can't? She can't what?" asks Kel.

"I can't go out with you, Kenan . . ." explains Amy, "because we have to move to Alaska right away. I'm sorry. Bye, Kenan." Amy gives Kenan a little kiss on the cheek, then walks back through the curtain, leaving him in a state of dismay.

"Now, that's inconvenient!" exclaims Kel.

"That's what *you* think!" says Kenan, with a big smile on his face.

Kel can tell Kenan has an idea and this worries him greatly. "Kenan! Why are you grinning like that? You're making my tummy hurt."

"You know, Kel," says Kenan, dreamily, "Alaska's not so far away."

Kel is becoming very upset. "Oh, but it is!" he argues. "It's way far away!"

"Kel! Grab some peanut butter and some snow shoes and meet me at the bus stop. You and me are Alaska bound."

"But, Kenan, I don't wanna go to Alaska. Besides, peanut butter aggravates my stomach. Can't we just stay in America?"

"I believe Alaska is part of America," replies Kenan.

"Oh yeah," says Kel. "I forgot."

"Now, Kel, you always said you wanted to meet an

Eskimo," says Kenan, putting his arm around Kel's shoulder. "They got lots of Eskimos up there in Alaska. This is gonna be your big chance."

"But, Kenan, I already met an Eskimo after our first adventure. Don't you remember? He was standin' right here on the stage. We were touching him and pulling on him."

"That's right," says Kenan, becoming more excited. "Maybe he'll let us spend a few nights with him. And if we can't, it's no big deal 'cause, like I said, they've got lots of Eskimos up in Alaska. And they've got snow, and ice, and polar bears, and penguins . . ."

"I don't think they have penguins," interrupts Kel.

"Well, okay, they don't have penguins, but you know what they *do* have?" asks Kenan.

"I don't care, Kenan," moans Kel.

"They've got *Amy!*" says Kenan, wrapping his arms around his own shoulders as if he were hugging her.

"Kenan, man, stop hugging yourself. They got plenty of girls right here in Chicago for you to be all in love with."

"I don't want other girls. I want Amy," says Kenan, and he walks away.

"Kenan? Kenan, where are you going?"

Kenan returns moments later wearing a parka, holding a suitcase and warm weather gear. "Come on, Kel. Let's go."

Kel is concerned. He can see how determined Kenan is to follow Amy up to Alaska. He thinks about how cold and uncomfortable he would be up there. *Sure,* he thinks. *I'll be with my pal, Kenan, but he'll be frozen solid. I've got to think of some way to talk Kenan out of this crazy idea.* Kel realizes he's never been able to talk Kenan out of anything before. Once Kenan gets an idea, it's all over. He must think of something quick, but what?

"Uh, hey, Kenan," Kel begins, "we just told the people about these three adventures, right?"

"Yeah," says Kenan. "So, what's your point?"

"Well, if you and me go to Alaska, what are the people gonna do? Who's gonna tell them about all of our other adventures?"

Kenan stops and considers this. "Yeah, I guess we owe it to the people."

"And besides," Kel continues, "how much trouble can guys like us get into in Alaska? It would get real boring after a while."

"Yeah," says Kenan. "And I'd still have to put up with Amy's angry daddy."

"That's true," agrees Kel. It worked! He's finally talked Kenan out of one of his ideas. Kel dances in a circle around Kenan.

"Okay, Kel. That's enough dancing," shouts Kenan. "It's time to thank the people for reading all about our adventures."

"I'm still not really understanding this, Kenan. Where are the people that we're thanking? I mean I'm used to having the TV cameras out there and all the people right here where you can see them."

"Trust me, Kel," says Kenan. "The people are there,

somewhere, and hopefully they'll be back to read about more of our adventures. And boy, have we got some adventures coming up!"

"Really?" asks Kel like a wide-eyed little boy. "Like what?"

"Well, Kel," says Kenan, "surely you don't expect me to tell you before I tell *them*. That wouldn't be very nice, would it? See you later everybody!"

And with that, Kenan walks away, leaving Kel confused and puzzled. "Nice? What are you talking about, Kenan?" asks Kel. "I'm nice, Kenan! Tell me, Kenan! What adventures are we gonna have next? Kenan? . . . Kenan? . . . Don't leave me here on the last page, Kenan!" Kel throws his hands across each other in disgust. "Aw, here it goes!" he says, and he runs off after Kenan.

ABOUT THE AUTHOR

STEVE FREEMAN is a Canada goose. A large water-fowl closely related to ducks and swans, he grazes mostly on vegetable matter, and is known to let out loud honking cries during migration. Not only is he the first goose to write a novelization, but he's the first *fowl of any kind* to own his own computer.